Ghost Town Secrets

Nicole Simon

Published by Nicole Simon, 2024.

This is a work of fiction. Similarities to real people, places, or events are entirely coincidental.

GHOST TOWN SECRETS

First edition. February 2, 2024.

Copyright © 2024 Nicole Simon.

ISBN: 979-8224655342

Written by Nicole Simon.

Ghost Town Secrets
A Western Romance Mystery

Nicole Simon

© Copyright 2024 - All rights reserved.

Chapter 1: Stranded in the Ghost Town

Emma could feel her head nodding to the rhythmic clopping of Cinnamon's hooves hitting the packed dirt. Whisps of strawberry blonde hair had escaped from underneath her hat, and she swatted at the strands listlessly. She was on day three of her solitary journey and had barely slept. The combination of the overcast sky and hot sun was making her drowsy. She blinked rapidly a few times and rubbed her bright blue eyes. She would take a break at the next town she came to, which didn't seem to be approaching any time soon based on the sparseness of the land around her. The road was reduced to hard packed dirt, and the fields on either side of her were barren. The grass was dry and brown, all of it overgrown. To her left, what looked like an old field of corn stood standing, but the stalks were dry and crunchy-looking. If she had to guess, those stalks had been left standing a few seasons past their last harvest.

Emma rubbed her eyes and blinked rapidly again. She paused, hand frozen in place, as what sounded like a crack underneath the wagon of her stagecoach punctuated the air over the clopping of Cinnamon's hooves. She looked at the horse, whose beautiful brown ears were perked up on her head. Cinnamon had definitely heard the noise as well. Emma told herself she just had to get to the next town, wherever that was.

"Keep it up, Cinnamon. Good girl," Emma cooed softly to the horse, who shook her mane as if to say, "I got this" and kept trotting forward.

Cinnamon had carried the stagecoach not too much farther when Emma heard the same cracking noise underneath the wagon, this time closer to the front. Emma gritted her teeth and hoped for a safe arrival in the next town. Just on the horizon, she could make out the outlines of a few buildings and what looked like a huge mansion on top of a hill, way off in the distance.

A faded sign on the side of the road, mostly hidden in the overgrown weeds, read "Onyx Falls- One Mile." Emma felt a weight lift from her shoulders, and she sat up straighter in her seat. The next town was only a mile away. Even if she did break down out here, she could unhitch Cinnamon and ride her into the town. She took another deep breath and shimmied backwards in her seat, which caused another cracking sound to emanate from underneath the wagon. Emma sat very still, holding the reigns, and barely moving her head to glance at her surroundings.

When Cinnamon's trots brought the wagon to the outskirts of town, Emma looked around in disbelief. This was not what she had hoped for as far as getting to the next town safely. This could barely be called a town. The road, packed hard with dirt, was threatened by an outcrop of weeds and flowers for as far as the eye could see. From what she could tell, this road continued straight through the town and clean to the other side. Buildings loomed on either side of the street, the faded paint chipped and peeling. Windows had been busted out sporadically in some of the buildings here and there, most of which had not been patched up or replaced.

"Easy, Cinnamon," Emma said, giving the reigns a light pull. The horse slowed down and tossed her head from side to side as if she too could not believe this was where they would be stopping.

The place was the very definition of a ghost town. All the storefronts looked like they had at one point been lively and bustling, and the cracked, slanted sidewalks proved that people had once needed to get from place to place in this town. The windows and doors were covered in a layer of dirt and dust. The dressmaker's shop still had mannequins in the window, dressed in a style Emma recognized from several years ago. She looked around in amazement, her bright blue eyes taking in the sight of what had once been a once beautiful place. The top of the general store had an ornate architectural design running across the roof. Several sections of this decorative piece were broken off, and the few shelves in the store that Emma could see had odds and ends of supplies-a few canned goods and what looked to be an opened sack of flour.

Emma was trying to peer into the dirty windows of the store to see if there was anything she could use when a curtain moved in the adjacent window. Her breath caught in her throat and she felt her face flush red, but she reminded herself that technically there was no crime in looking in a store window, and certainly no crime in looking in the window of a store that was no longer in operation. The curtain twitched again, and Emma pulled on Cinnamon's reigns to make her stop.

The horse halted, then stomped her foot and let out a huff of indignation.

"I know, I know," Emma said. "I don't think it's worth stopping here either."

Emma wasn't entirely sure she believed herself. She had just seen the curtain move, right? Surely that meant someone was here? Someone living in this ghost town was definitely better than the alternative option, which was ghosts and spirits living in these abandoned buildings. She stared at the faded red checked curtains, then let her eyes drift upwards. The sign on the building read "Maverick's Saloon." Most of the letters in the name had faded, making the sign look at first glance like "Ma's Saloon," which made her smile.

The curtain moved back and a face appeared in the window. Emma felt her cheeks redden again, this time with embarrassment that she had been caught grinning at the seemingly vacant building. The curtain fell back and the door next to it opened immediately. Out stepped a tall man wearing cowboy boots, brown pants, and an apron. He was handsome in a rugged way, with dark shaggy hair and a five o'clock shadow of a beard on his face. He had a small scar on his left cheek, a half-moon that was barely visible. He nodded to Emma and took two steps to the front of the porch, then stepped down to the ground.

"May I?" he asked, gesturing toward Cinnamon.

"Of course," Emma said.

She watched the man hold his hand out toward Cinnamon, who sniffed him cautiously, then leaned her big brown head forward to nuzzle him.

"I'm Jack," he said, looking toward Emma and giving a little wave.

"I'm Emma," she responded, nodding at him and touching the brim of her felt hat. She searched her mind frantically for something intelligent to say, but "what are you doing in that building" and "I thought this town was abandoned" didn't sound very friendly.

"Just passing through?" Jack asked.

"Yes. I'm on my way to take a reporting job."

"I figured as much. Onyx Falls isn't really a destination stop anymore," he said, grinning at her apologetically.

"Well, I did wonder if it was abandoned," Emma admitted. She was normally very composed and able to keep up with change in conversation, but found herself not capable of forming a complete, intelligent sentence in front of this handsome stranger and his intense, piercing blue eyes.

Jack smiled. "A lot of people have moved on and the town has seen better days, but we do still have some great establishments left, like my very own Maverick's Saloon," he said, turning sideways and gesturing dramatically.

Emma glanced politely up at the building and smoothed her dress over her knees.

"And the Bennett Inn," he added, pointing across the street to an old building that Emma had assumed to be vacant.

While the scenery in the small Montana town looked gorgeous, Emma was not sure this was the place she wanted to stay for the evening. Did that old inn even have sheets that had been changed this year or floors that could be trusted to be walked across?

"I make the best steak this side of the Rockies," Jack said, winking at her. "Why don't you at least come in for a meal and give ol' girl here a rest?"

Emma smiled down at him from her seat on the stagecoach.

Jack smiled back at her, and she couldn't resist noticing his perfectly straight white teeth and bright blue eyes. She briefly forgot about the job waiting for her and the long journey she would have to finish in order to get there.

"Well, I am a little hungry," Emma mumbled, blushing.

"Perfect," Jack said, offering his hand up to help her step down.

She placed her dainty hand in his and allowed him to help her down. As soon as she stepped foot on the ground, the stagecoach creaked, another problem she had momentarily forgotten in the wake of the handsome cowboy's charming smile.

Jack looked back at the stagecoach, then at Cinnamon. "That doesn't sound good," he mused. He dropped Emma's hand and crouched down under the wagon, then quickly scurried backwards. "The front axle is about to snap," he said matter-of-factly. "It's a good thing you stopped when you did. We need to get your horse unhitched."

Emma's stomach dropped at the thought of anything happening to Cinnamon, and she quickly went to work undoing the reigns and harness. Jack unhooked the singletree while Emma led the horse forward. Suddenly there was a loud cracking sound. The front axle of the stagecoach had split completely in half, the two parts falling inward and resting on the ground directly below where she had just been sitting.

Emma's breath caught in her throat as she thought about what could have happened to her or Cinnamon if the axle had broken just a mile back in their journey.

"Oh, poor girl," she murmured, rubbing the horse's nose with one hand and running her fingers through her mane with the other.

"It can be fixed, but unfortunately not for a few days," Jack reassured her. "We don't exactly get deliveries quickly." He moved his hands in a sweeping motion in front of himself, as if to demonstrate the state of the town.

Emma nodded, still a little shaken up.

"In the meantime, I can set up your horse in my stable," Jack jerked his thumb over his shoulder, gesturing to the stable behind the saloon.

"Sure, that would be great," Emma agreed, grateful for the chance to rest and a voice of reason to help decide what her next steps should be.

"In the meantime, you can head into the saloon and make yourself at home."

Emma smoothed down the front of her dress and nodded. "Thank you."

She headed towards the wooden porch of the saloon, opening the door slowly and letting her eyes adjust to the dark surroundings. There was a bar running along the length of one of the walls, with mismatched barstools waiting for patrons. Three wanted posters hung behind the bar, but it was too dark for Emma to make out the photos. Several tables were scattered throughout the dining room area. Emma wasn't sure where to sit. The tables were all in the shadows, and she wanted to be close to the door, so perhaps sitting at the bar might be the better option. She wondered if that was an appropriate place for a woman.

Emma decided to choose to sit at the bar and had just dusted off a seat and sat down when Jack walked back in.

"A lady who sits at the bar. I like it," he called, walking through the door that connected the kitchen to the bar.

Emma smiled at him and graciously accepted the glass of water he handed her.

"I got your horse all set up in the stable with fresh hay and a full trough of water."

"Thank you," Emma said. "I really appreciate it."

"Of course," Jack said. "I also got a steak started for you."

Emma smiled gratefully and took a long drink of water.

While they waited for the steak to cook, the two made small talk. Emma told Jack about the newspaper reporting job she was taking in California and her parents and two older siblings. Jack told Emma about his parents, whom he had lost at a young age, and his sister, wo lived in the neighboring town. He told her about how the town was once busy and lively, and even though people had begun to leave at a rapid rate, he still held out hope that things could be saved.

An hour flew by, and Emma suddenly straightened in her seat when she realized the already dark saloon had grown even darker. The sun had almost set and the street looked even more ominous than it had when her stagecoach rolled into town amidst the overcast sky. She wasn't sure what to do. Obviously traveling in a stagecoach with a broken axle was out of the question, and there was no way Cinnamon could carry all her belongings for the move halfway across the country.

As if Jack could read her mind, he said, "Let me call over to the Bennett Inn. They can get you set up until we can get that axle fixed."

Emma felt a twinge of reassurance at Jack's use of the word "we."

"Thank you," she said for what felt like the millionth time that day. "That would be great."

As the two went out to the porch, Jack locked the doors of the saloon behind them, which Emma found peculiar considering there didn't seem to be many people in the town. The two walked to the hotel across the street, still keeping up their easy conversation.

Once they stepped inside the inn, Emma looked around in awe at the ornate building. The beautiful interior was a complete contrast to the run-down exterior. The polished hardwood floors of the lobby shined brightly under the soft overhead lights. The walls were painted a cream color, and plush arm chairs sat aside a walnut parlor table. Heavy drapes lined all of the windows that overlooked the streets, which made

Emma temporarily forget that just on the other side of those drapes was a desolate looking town.

"Wow," Emma breathed, taking in the room. "This is gorgeous."

"I know," Jack agreed, chuckling softly as he watched Emma take in her surroundings. "Not quite what you would expect based on what you see outside. Sarah does a great job of keeping this place in tip top shape."

Emma took a few paces forward, relishing the sound of the creaking floor beneath her, which was similar to that of her childhood home. She rang the little bell that was sitting on the table, and at the merry tinkling sound, a woman appeared around the corner as if by magic. The woman seemed to fit right in with the welcoming atmosphere of the hotel. She was pleasant looking in a grandmotherly sort of way and her graying hair was swept back in a bun. She wore an apron over a long dress, as if Emma and Jack had just interrupted an evening cookie-baking session. Her eyes lit up when she saw them, and she immediately came from behind the counter to introduce herself.

She grasped Emma's outstretched hand and smiled brightly while Jack introduced the two women and recounted the evening's events.

"Oh my goodness," Sarah responded after Jack finished his tale. "Of course there is room for you here at Bennett Inn. Any friend of Jack's is certainly welcome here for as long as you need to stay."

"Thank you," Emma responded. She definitely needed to come up with a better repertoire of responses to express her gratitude for the kindness of the residents in this town.

"Of course," Sarah said, reaching out to grasp Emma's arm. "I can set you up on the large master suite on the second floor. It's the best room here."

"Thank you, Sarah," Jack said. He turned to Emma. "I'll let you get settled in. Tomorrow we can take a look at that stagecoach axle. For now, Cinnamon is safe in the stable, and you are in good hands with Sarah."

Jack nodded to each of the women, put on his cowboy hat, and made his way out the door into the night. To where, Emma had no idea. The saloon? The stable? From outward appearances, there seemed to be no functional buildings in this town, but as she learned from the saloon and the stable, appearances could be deceiving.

"You have had quite a day, young lady," Sarah said, looking at Emma kindly. "Let's get you set up. Follow me."

Emma followed Sarah up the wide staircase and into the hallway on the second floor. Plush carpet lined the floor, and flowered wallpaper decorated the walls, from floor to very tall ceiling. The dim lights cast long shadows on the walls, giving the otherwise welcoming hallway a spooky vibe. Sarah stopped at a door and reached in her apron to pull out a ring of keys.

"This is the best room here, in my opinion," she said, opening the door and allowing Emma to enter first.

Emma could see why Sarah thought that. The room was huge, with a large fluffy mattress and several quilts on the bed. There were tall windows on three sides of the room, and a bathroom with a large clawfoot tub and stacks of towels. A lamp in the corner cast a soft glow over the room.

"It's beautiful," Emma said in amazement. "Thank you so much."

"You can stay as long as you need to," Sarah said, turning towards the door. "My room is on the third floor. You are welcome to walk around the second floor and the common areas on the first floor. The first floor has a library and a dining room. Breakfast is at seven," she said, shutting the door behind her.

Emma walked over to the bed and ran her hand along the edge of the mattress. It felt so soft and cozy. She decided to lay down for just a little bit before getting ready to go to sleep.

Suddenly, Emma sat up and looked around in confusion. It took her a few seconds to process where she was. She had only intended to rest for a minute before getting ready for bed, but apparently had fallen asleep. She rubbed her eyes and listened for any movement in the building, but the place was eerily silent. Emma crossed the room to the bathroom and washed her face, then changed clothes and crawled into bed. She lay under the covers for an indefinite amount of time, tossing and turning. The grandfather clock in the corner showed three o'clock, then three thirty, then four. Sighing, Emma gingerly placed one foot on the hardwood floor, then the other. She was never going to be able to go back to sleep at this rate. Somehow the silence was actually making it harder to sleep. She crept out of bed and tiptoed around the room. She pulled the drapes back and looked down at the abandoned street. A lone newspaper blew down the street in the breeze. Emma shuddered. Despite the friendliness of Sarah and Jack, the town still had a creepy, almost haunting atmosphere.

Against the wall adjacent to the bed stood a large wardrobe. Emma opened the doors to inspect the area where she would be able to hang her clothes tomorrow when she brought her belongings inside. She had a feeling she would be stuck here for longer than she originally expected. There was no way the axle could be fixed in time for her to make it to California by next week. Sighing, Emma was about to close the door to the wardrobe when something caught her eye. She bent down to inspect the object, which turned out to be a small book of some sort. She probably would have missed it, except for the fact that the draperies had not fallen completely shut after she looked outside, and the moon was casting a sliver of light through the open drapes and into the doors of the wardrobe. Emma felt the soft cover and frowned. A journal maybe? How would it have gotten here? She pulled the book out and brought it closer to the window. It was a journal whose dark cover would make it easy to miss in the back of the wardrobe when someone was packing their belongings or coming in to clean the day after this guest left. Emma sat in a chair by the window and gingerly fanned the pages open. It was definitely a female's writing with loopy curling letters in a heavy-handed scrawl. Emma flipped to the back page and gasped, dropping the diary. The last two sentences read "He was never in love with me. If you find this, please he..." The last two letters of what Emma assumed would complete the word "help" were never formed by the writer.

Chapter 2: Uncovering Clues

Emma stared at the diary for what seemed like minutes, but in reality, was only several seconds. In the fall from her hand to the floor, the diary had closed and landed on its back cover. The word "diary" was scrawled across the front in gold gilt letters, atop a dark brown leather cover. Emma reached down hesitantly and picked the diary up off the floor, fanning the pages again. She looked around her room. What else could be hidden here? She opened the chest of drawers and swept her hand over the floor of the wardrobe again, just to make sure she hadn't missed anything else. There was nothing. Emma sat on the edge of the bed, still clutching the small book.

Emma opened the front cover and saw a woman's name written in the same loopy scrawl that could be found inside the pages. The name read Isabel Monroe. Emma frowned and flipped through the diary again. The name didn't mean anything to her, but then again, she was a stranger in this town and until last night, had not known anyone here until she happened upon Jack and the saloon, and as a result, Sarah and the inn. Emma laid the diary on the bed next to her and crossed the room to the bathroom. There was no way she could go back to sleep now. As she washed her face and combed her hair, she found her mind wandering to Jack. How could he stay here in this town? Yes, he owned the saloon, but he was young, about her age or a little older, and surely he had plans to get married and have a family? She blushed as she thought of him smiling at her yesterday when she agreed to let him cook her a steak. Emma was about to head downstairs when, on second thought, she rouged her cheeks and sprayed a hint of perfume on her neck, just in case she ran into Jack today.

Just a few minutes before seven, Emma took her seat at the long table in the dining room. The scent of maple syrup wafted out from the kitchen, as she sat flipping through the diary, trying to ascertain some clues about this Isabel woman. From what she could tell, Isabel was about Emma's age, in her mid-twenties, and seemed to have a lot of money. The first part of the diary talked about a lavish trip to Europe and some new expensive dresses she was having shipped. Emma had just gotten to an entry that talked about how Isabel was afraid someone was stalking her when Sarah came out of the kitchen holding two plates heaped full of pancakes, eggs, and sausage, which she set down on the table.

"Good morning," Sarah half sang, half spoke to Emma. "I hope you don't mind if I join you for breakfast since you're my only tenant."

Emma smiled. "Of course I don't mind. I'd love for you to join me."

Sarah let out a huff as she sat in the chair across from Emma. She arranged her food on her plate and poured syrup from an antique porcelain carafe onto the pile of pancakes on her plate. She took one bite and closed her eyes, savoring the taste, and then looked over at Emma, as if she forgot she was technically the host.

"What are you reading?" she asked curiously.

Emma's hand flew protectively to the cover of the diary. She had looked forward to showing this to Sarah and Jack since she had read the last line, but now for some reason, she was having second thoughts. She glanced up at Sarah, who had paused, fork in the air, looking directly at her. Her round, pleasant face showed nothing but patience, and her kind eyes crinkled in the corner when she smiled. Emma took a deep breath.

"Well, I actually found this in the bottom of the wardrobe earlier. It seems to be an old diary." Emma said as she showed it to Sarah.

"Oh wow. I'll be," Sarah mused. "I bet someone is missing that. Is there a name? Maybe we can get it back to its rightful owner somehow."

"Well, that's the thing," Emma started. She looked over at Sarah again, whose face still only showed kindness as she scooped a bite of pancakes into her mouth, chewing quietly. Emma flipped to the final page and started to tell what she had found. "The last entry is really spooky. It looks like the person was asking for help but never actually got to finish the rest of her sentence."

Sarah put her fork down. "What? Are you sure?"

Emma held the diary up for her to see. Sarah squinted and pulled the diary closer to her face. Her eyes widened when she read the last line.

Emma studied Sarah's shocked face for a few seconds, then continued. "Apparently this diary belongs to some lady named Isabel. Does that ring a bell?"

Sarah's fork clattered to her plate and she let out an audible gasp. "Isabel? As in Isabel Monroe?" Her hand flew to her neck where a heart pendant hung on a chain. She began to play with the necklace, moving the heart back and forth across the chain with one hand.

"I think that was the name that was written in the front?" Emma posed this as a question, even though she was sure that was the name she had read. She flipped to the front of the diary to confirm, and then looked up and nodded her head. She had no idea who this mysterious Isabel Monroe person was. How did Sarah instantly know who the diary belonged to? And why was she so visibly nervous? Emma frowned and studied Sarah carefully across the table. Her eyes were still wide and she looked like she had seen a ghost.

Sarah reached her hand towards the diary. "May I?"

Emma handed Sarah the small book, and she flipped to the first page. "Oh my goodness. This definitely belongs to her."

As if it was poisoned, she hurriedly shoved the diary back across the table at Emma, who stared at her quizzically, still clueless as to who Isabel Monroe actually was, other than someone who Sarah clearly knew and who apparently needed help of some kind.

"Isabel inherited a huge fortune from a family who had ties to some Native American wealth. Shortly after she inherited the money, she disappeared. Jack and I suspected something awful had happened to her, but others thought she had simply taken the money and left. But that just wasn't like her. She was from here. This had been her lifelong home," Sarah said quietly.

Emma couldn't imagine that someone from this deserted place actually had the kind of money that would attract kidnappers, but then again, she also hadn't expected this hotel to be operable, so she had a feeling there were a lot of things she didn't know about this town and its inhabitants.

"Wow," Emma said. "So, what do *you* think happened to her?"

Sarah continued to play with the locket around her neck. She glanced around, even though she and Emma were the only two in the dining room. "I always said she would have never just disappeared. She had recently started dating someone in town and would never have just left him. She was head over heels for that man! I never understood it because he was old enough to be her father, but he certainly had a hold on her."

Emma leaned forward in her seat. Sarah had her full attention now. "Do you think she is alive still?"

Sarah's eyes filled with tears. "I don't know. She's been missing for about three months now. She just vanished, seemingly overnight. Her family played a huge part in founding this town."

"Wait a minute," Emma said, flipping the diary back to the last page again. "I think she mentions him on this page here." Emma read Sarah the line she had read when she first found the diary: "He was never in love with me."

All the color drained from Sarah's face. "Oh my goodness," she said softly. "That poor girl."

Emma pursed her lips and nodded in agreement. She had no idea where to go from here. Would the diary really hold clues to what had happened to this missing woman, or would all the entries be about Isabel's love affair with this mysterious older man?

The two women sat in stunned silence for a few seconds. Emma looked at the clock in the corner. It was after eight o'clock already. She was going to have to figure out how to fix the axle on her stagecoach, and she wanted to check on Cinnamon this morning.

Just then, the little bell jingled in the lobby, followed by a voice calling out, "It's just me!"

Emma recognized the voice as Jack's, and her hands flew to her hair to pat everything into place. She blushed when she caught Sarah looking at her with a knowing smile.

"We're in the dining room!" Sarah called out.

Jack came through the doorway of the dining room and smiled directly at Emma.

"Good morning, ladies," he said as he pulled out a chair at the table. "Do you mind if I join you?"

Sarah glanced over at Emma, giving her a surreptitious wink. "Why Jack, what a nice surprise. I haven't had the pleasure of your company at breakfast for quite some time."

Jack ran his hands through his dark hair and avoided looking at either Sarah or Emma as he busied himself with unrolling his napkin and arranging his silverware. "I thought I might need a hearty breakfast so I can get this wagon axle fixed."

"Of course," Sarah nodded knowingly, standing up from the table. "I'll get you a plate fixed. In the meantime, Emma has some news for you."

"Oh?" Jack asked, raising his eyebrows, and turning towards Emma. "Is that so?"

She blushed as he turned his full attention toward her, then busied herself finding the last page in the diary, which she showed him, then flipped to the front page that showed the diary belonged to Isabel.

Jack let out a low whistle. "Where did you get this?"

Emma recounted finding the diary in the wardrobe and searching for any other left-behind items but finding nothing.

Jack stared at her in stunned silence for what seemed like forever, his blue eyes boring into hers.

"Do you think she's still alive?" Emma asked softly.

Jack pursed his lips and opened his mouth as if to answer but let a look of relief wash over him when Sarah returned from the kitchen carrying a plate of pancakes and a mug of coffee. She set the items on the table and then returned to her seat, looking back and forth between Emma and Jack.

"Should we notify Sheriff Campbell?" Sarah asked.

Jack sighed. Emma thought notifying a figure of authority seemed like the logical thing to do, but she noticed Jack seemed hesitant.

"I think we should talk to Ezekial before we do anything," Jack responded slowly.

Sarah nodded. "Zeke would probably know more of the back story."

Emma looked from Jack to Sarah.

"Who is Ezekial?" she asked.

"He's our unofficial town detective," Jack said with a chuckle. "Old Zeke has been here longer than any of us, and he knows every detail about each family. Think gossipy old lady but in male form."

Emma smiled. "Sounds like we should start with him."

"Zeke usually comes in for lunch. Let's go out to the stable and look at this wagon axle while we wait for him," Jack said.

Emma sipped her coffee and fell into an easy conversation with Jack. Sarah watched them with a knowing look as they said goodbye to her and walked out the front door of the inn.

Once they got to the stable, Emma went straight to Cinnamon's stall and nuzzled the horse. "What have we gotten ourselves into, sweet girl?" she whispered. The horse burrowed her head into Emma's shoulder. She was brushing Cinnamon's mane when Jack came back in with the two pieces of the stagecoach's axle. He set them on the ground and frowned.

"This might take a little more work than I thought," he said.

Emma went over to the center aisle and stood next to Jack. He pointed to a piece that connected the wagon wheel to the axle. The metal was bent haphazardly.

"This piece will have to be ordered and shipped, so it might take a few days," he told her.

Emma nodded, then looked over at Cinnamon, who stood in her stall. If she had to break down, she couldn't have asked for a better place for it to happen. But what had she gotten herself into with this diary and the missing woman? She had only wanted to stop and stretch her legs and get a meal and then be on her merry way to start the new job.

"Well, I guess now I have something to do for the next few days until the axle can be fixed," Emma said, waving the diary in the air.

Jack raised his eyebrows. "We might need your investigative journalism skills here."

The two made their way to the saloon, where Emma could hear the sounds of plates clattering in the kitchen.

"Nancy!" Jack called. "It's just me!"

Emma felt a little jealous pang at the mention of this Nancy person, then quickly reminded herself that it didn't matter who Nancy was because she was leaving in a few days for a completely different state to start her new job.

A strawberry-blonde haired woman flounced out of the kitchen, dish towel in hand.

"Hi, Jack!" she sang out, then stopped short. "Hi there! I'm Nancy!"

Emma introduced herself, and Jack then recounted the story for the second time of how she wound up in their town.

"Oh, good grief," gushed Nancy. "You've had a busy twenty-four hours."

Emma smiled. "You could say that."

"Well please have a seat. I'm preparing lunch for the locals. By now I'm sure Ezekial has somehow learned you're here and will be in anytime," Nancy joked.

Emma's smile grew wider. She could tell already that she was going to like Nancy. Right on cue, the door opened, and a tall man shuffled in. He was holding a folder under one arm and walking in a stooped manner, as if constantly waiting for this folder of papers to slip out of his grasp. He looked disheveled, with wrinkled clothing and a graying, unkempt beard, but his eyes were kind as he looked at Emma.

"Well, hello there," he said, offering his hand out to her. "I'm Zeke. You must be Emma."

Nancy swatted at Zeke with the towel she was holding and let out a lighthearted, girly laugh. "You just made my little joke a reality, Zeke."

Zeke smiled. "I happened to see Sarah out on the front porch on my way over. I saw the stagecoach parked here yesterday on my late-night walk and could only assume that its driver would have stayed at the inn."

"Well, you know we're always happy to see you. Lunch is almost ready," Nancy said, heading back to the kitchen.

"Okay," Ezekial said, smiling as he pulled out a chair and sat down at one of the tables.

With the new introductions, Emma had almost forgotten about the diary she was holding in her hand. It was mostly concealed by the folds of her skirt, and apparently no one else had noticed what she was holding either. She held the diary up and looked at Jack questioningly. He nodded and pulled out a chair next to Ezekial.

"Zeke, Emma has something to show you," he said, gesturing for Emma to sit down at the table. "We have reason to believe Isabel is still alive."

Ezekial raised his eyebrows and looked at Jack. "That's great news! What makes you say that? It seemed like we reached a dead end."

Jack looked over at Emma, waiting for her to continue the story. She brought out the diary, and for the third time that day, flipped to the last page and then back to the name in the front. Ezekial squinted, then pulled some wire-frame glasses out of his suit pocket. Emma sat perched on the edge of her seat as she watched him unfold the glasses, rest the glasses on his nose, then readjust the glasses and finally read the lines in the book. He flipped back and forth between the last entry in the book and the front page a few times. Emma looked over at Jack, who looked at Ezekial, back to Emma, and then grinned. Emma smiled as she realized that Jack thought Ezekial was being dramatic.

Finally, Ezekial spoke. "I never liked Thomas. Even when we were kids, he was just so mean."

"The man Isabel is talking about in the diary is Thomas Benson," Jack explained. "Thomas and Zeke here grew up together."

"And Thomas was way too old for her," Nancy interjected, plunking a plate of fried chicken down in the middle of the table. "She could have done better than him."

"Yes," grumbled Ezekial. "And she had money, so she didn't need him. That relationship made no sense. What does the diary say?"

"I just found it this morning," Emma said. "I haven't really gotten a chance to read anything yet."

Emma opened the diary to the first entry, and Ezekial, Jack, and Nancy crowded around her as she read out loud.

"January first. Thomas called on me today. I always viewed him as one of Daddy's boring business partners, but he came to check on me since he knew I was here by myself during the blizzard. He made sure I had food and water and brought the most beautiful poinsettia."

"Stop right there!" Ezekial cried. "What was the date of that entry again?"

"January first," Emma said.

"Well, okay," Ezekial muttered. "Go on."

Emma continued reading, "This has been the longest winter, so it was nice to have some company and to be thought of. He said he would check back in on me next week. I told him how much I appreciated it, because ever since last summer, I've been so terribly lonely."

Emma paused. "She sounds so sad. What happened to her?"

"She was engaged to a man who was Native American. His name was Dakota," Nancy said. "He died in a tragic accident which was rather weird. No one knows how but he fell into an abandoned mine and his neck was broken. It was Isabel who found him."

Emma set the diary on the table, but Ezekial spoke up before she could say anything. "Yes, an 'accident,' that's what they say," his voice inflection changed at the word "accident."

"Now, we don't know that there was any foul play," Nancy admonished him.

"Well, we don't know that there wasn't, either," Ezekial said, one finger pointing in the air to emphasize his point.

Emma picked up the diary again and read, "I can't wait to see him next week."

"Oh, bullocks," Ezekial grumbled. He stood and collected his folder of papers. "Nancy, the food was delicious as always. Emma, it was nice to meet you. I'm heading back to the office for a bit and going to see what I can dig up about Thomas."

Jack, Emma, and Nancy watched Ezekial walk out the front door and into the dusty streets. A few stray leaves and an old newspaper floated by in the breeze as if they were chasing after him.

Nancy was the first to break the silence. "Don't pay him no mind," she advised Emma. "Zeke is hell-bent on proving that Thomas is corrupt. He's worse than a gossipy old lady, but we love him," she laughed.

"By this time tomorrow he'll have a whole theory mapped out and will have everyone's family tree on paper," Jack added.

"He could be on to something though," Emma offered. "Why would Thomas suddenly take an interest in her? He sounds like he was just a boring old man who her father did business with."

"I think that originally what he intended to be was just an old associate of her father's who went to check in on her. But when he got there, he saw this lonely, beautiful woman who was no longer a child and that's when he fell for her," Nancy said. "Or he found an easy target, if you listen to Ezekial."

Both women looked at Jack. "Let's keep reading," he suggested.

Just then the saloon door burst open, and a large man loomed in the doorway. With the sun shining behind him, all Emma could see was his shadow. He stood in the doorway for longer than necessary, surveying his surroundings. Jack grabbed the diary from Emma and placed it on his lap, slowly scooted his chair closer to the table, and resumed eating. The man sauntered over to the table, seeming to revel in the fact that everyone was watching him as his cowboy boots clicked against the hardwood floor. Not wasting time with pleasantries, he addressed Jack as soon as he got to the table. "Hello there, Jack. I see you found yourself a new customer today."

"Thomas, this is Emma. She'll be staying at the inn for a few days until her stagecoach can get repaired," said Jack.

Emma reached out her hand, and Thomas took her dainty hand in his large one. His grip was firm in an unfriendly way, and she felt a chill run through her when he smiled. She quickly retracted her hand and placed it in her lap.

"It's nice to meet you," she said to Thomas, but his attention was already focused elsewhere.

"Jack," Thomas said, turning his full attention towards him. "I've been speaking with Ezekial. You know he keeps meticulous records of everything that has happened in this town since its founding."

Emma looked at Jack, who seemed to be just as puzzled as she was.

"Oh, come on, Thomas. We all know Zeke keeps these records," Nancy laughed nervously. "He just left here with a folder under his arm. You're going to have to try harder than that to bring us some news."

Thomas didn't smile. "I've gone over the records dating back to when the town was first founded. Your grandfather didn't pay taxes on this saloon the first year it was opened. Therefore, Benson Enterprises can own this building by the end of the month if we pay the back taxes, which I am fully prepared to do."

Chapter 3: Haunted Past

Emma stood near the edge of the lake, looking at her new yellow dress in the reflection. The water was peaceful and serene, but she could sense danger in the pit of her stomach. Clouds were building up overhead and thunder rumbled in the distance. The leaves on the trees had flipped over, showing their silver undersides. Jenny, her best friend, should have been standing next to her with her reflection visible in the lake too, right next to Emma's. The girls had been inseparable since their parents moved next door to each other and had done everything together. They walked to school together, they bought penny candy at Christmas together, and played dolls by the lake together. Where was Jenny?

"Emma! Emma!" her mother's frantic voice pierced the humid air.

Emma bolted upright in the bed and looked around frantically, trying to slow her breathing as the items in the room came into focus and she realized where she was. The porcelain water pitcher sat on the walnut table in the corner. The embroidered tapestry on the wall and the wardrobe let her know she was safe in her room at Bennett Inn. Her dreams always seemed so real, and were exactly how events had happened in life, right down to the leaves on the trees and the thunder in the distance. She got up slowly and walked to the bathroom to splash water on her face. A glance at the clock revealed it was almost dinner time and that her nap lasted longer than intended.

Earlier that day, Emma had gone back to her room to think about the morning's troubling events. The talk of the missing woman and then Thomas Benson who just showed up out of nowhere had put her nerves on edge. This seemingly abandoned ghost town had people lurking in every corner.

She was likely going to be here for a few more days at least. After lunch Jack had sent word to the blacksmith to request a new connector piece and had also sent word to a mill a few miles away. Both places said their respective parts would take at least four days to arrive, then there was the business of actually using the parts to fix the stagecoach. Emma had come back to her room to rest for a bit and write a letter to her parents to let them know where she was, but she must have been more tired than she realized.

Emma made her way downstairs into the parlor and settled herself into an overly stuffed floral-patterned armchair that sat directly in a ray of late afternoon sunshine. She pulled out the diary and began to read the next entry.

January 7th

As promised, Thomas has come back to check on me. He is sweet and thoughtful, and it is so nice to have someone to talk to again. I've been here all week by myself, with only my cat for company. I started a quilt, and Thomas even expressed interest in my quilt design. He brought me a tin of chocolates, and since the snow finally melted, we were able to take a long walk through the garden.

Emma set the diary on her lap and stared out the window. The picture that Isabel was painting in her diary of this Thomas Benson was vastly different from the Thomas Benson that she had met earlier that afternoon. He had seemed arrogant and brash and had threatened to take over the saloon. She tried to imagine this same man bringing chocolates to a woman and walking through a garden but couldn't picture it happening. Emma opened the diary again and continued reading.

January 9th

Thomas came to call on me again today, and we went on a carriage ride through the countryside. When we arrived back home, he kissed me! Admittedly I didn't feel the fireworks like when Dakota used to kiss me, but it sure was nice to have a safe companion. Thomas said he would call on me again this weekend.

Emma frowned and closed the diary again. The general consensus was that Isabel had really been in love with this man, but the diary painted a different picture. She seemed lonely and in search of a companion after Dakota was tragically taken from her. Emma closed her eyes. The pain of losing someone unexpectedly was a feeling that never fully went away, but instead felt different over time. She thought of the dream she had earlier and got a chill. She too had lost someone unexpectedly, although it was a much different relationship than what Isabel and Dakota had.

The door to the parlor swung open and she looked up to see Sarah bustling through, carrying a tray of cookies and two glasses of milk.

"Hello," the kind woman sang out in her soothing voice. "I thought you might want a snack. Dinner will be ready soon. Have you found anything else out?"

Emma felt her eyes fill with tears and her chin start to quiver. When Sarah pulled a handkerchief out of her dress pocket and passed it to her, she couldn't stop the tears from falling.

"There, there. My goodness," Sarah said soothingly. She placed a hand on Emma's shoulder and waited until Emma could compose herself. "What has brought all this on?'

Emma wiped her eyes. "I'm sorry," she said, shaking her head.

"Don't be sorry. Something is clearly upsetting you." Sarah sat down in the armchair and waited patiently for her to speak.

Emma sniffled and sat up straighter in her chair. "When I was younger, I had a friend named Jenny." She smiled at the memory, and Sarah nodded her head in encouragement.

"Well, we were about ten years old when this happened," Emma continued. "We used to walk to and from school together. We'd stop at the lake on the way home and feed the ducks our scraps from lunch. One day I stayed home from school because I had a fever. That was the day Jenny never came home from school. Authorities searched everywhere. The lake, our houses, the whole town. She was never found."

Emma stared at her hands in her lap, lost in thought. Finally, Sarah broke the silence.

"Oh, honey," she said.

Emma looked up to see Sarah toying with the locket on her necklace.

"Yeah," Emma said. "Right before I came downstairs, I woke up from a dream. It was so real, just like the events that happened. I was standing at the lake and could hear my mother calling my name to come home. Then I woke up."

"Our minds can do some crazy things," Sarah said. She continued moving the locket back and forth across its chain.

"I think about Jenny a lot. What would she be doing now? Would she be married? Would she have kids? And how could she just have disappeared? I think that's a huge reason for me to go into investigative journalism. Jenny was never found, but maybe I can be of assistance somehow to other families."

Sarah smiled. "I think that's a wonderful reason to choose your career. I can see you being a source of comfort to families in times like that."

"I guess this diary has really brought a lot of that back up. Jenny's family didn't have anyone to help them, other than the authorities. The detectives certainly weren't very friendly," said Emma.

"I know you're only here for a short time," Sarah began, somewhat hesitantly. "But maybe you could help us solve the mystery of Isabel. This diary gives me hope that she might be still out there somewhere."

Emma smiled. "I'll do whatever I can to help while I'm here."

Sarah stood up from her chair, and likewise, so did Emma. Sarah extended her plump arms in a motherly hug, and Emma accepted, grateful for the comfort.

"Let's go eat!" Sarah boomed.

Emma tossed and turned that night, and when it was time to wake up, she realized she almost slept through breakfast. She hurriedly got up and applied the bare minimum of makeup, then flipped through her dresses, settling on the blue one that accented her eyes.

When she got to the dining room, she was surprised to see not only Jack and Sarah there, but Nancy and Ezekial too. She took her place at the table and gratefully accepted the cup of coffee Sarah poured for her.

"We've all been talking about the diary," Nancy said by way of good morning. "We really want to find Isabel."

Emma nodded. "I'll be here for a few days and would love to help you all."

Everyone began to toss out various theories as to who could have been behind the kidnapping and why. Emma felt herself staring into space, as the feelings of fear and confusion she felt as a child echoed in the words of those at the table. She remembered sitting in the parlor with her mother, both of them on the couch, while the investigators sat across from them in two armchairs. The stern men, wearing dark suits and serious expressions, asked Emma the same questions over and over again: What route did you always take home from school? Where would she have detoured if you were not there? When was the last time you actually saw her?

"Emma! Earth to Emma!" Jack called to her across the table.

Blushing, Emma shook her head and brought herself back to the present. "I'm sorry," she said. "I was just thinking about something." Out of the corner of her eye, she saw Sarah watching her, and knew she was thinking about their conversation from yesterday.

"I can tell," Jack said kindly. "We were talking about how we need to read through the diary to see if we can find any other clues. How could the diary have even gotten here in the first place? Sarah said Isabel never stayed at the inn."

Emma looked over at Sarah, who nodded her head in agreement.

"Wait!" Nancy called out. "Didn't someone associated with Thomas Benson stay here for a night?" She looked around at the rest of the table. "Remember? He was traveling through on a business trip or something. We all thought it was fishy that he would stay here, only one town over from where he lives. I think we just avoided him when he was here."

"Yes, but wasn't that before Isabel went missing?" Ezekial asked.

The table speculated for a bit on whether the mystery man had stayed at the hotel before or after Isabel disappeared.

"Come on, Zeke," Nancy joked. "Check your archives. You know you have this written down somewhere."

Sarah let out a chuckle. "You have a more accurate log of who has stayed here than my own hotel registry."

Zeke smiled, a twinkle in his eye. "See? Being meticulous will finally pay off."

Emma looked around the table at Jack, Nancy, Sarah, and Ezekial. She might not have been able to help Jenny, but she could use her time and energy while she was here to help this unlikely crew of people find the person *they* knew and loved.

Chapter 4: Saloon Showdown

Emma was sitting at the bar of the saloon later that day, speculating about what could have happened to Isabel. She and Jack and Nancy were passing the diary around, alternating turns at reading out loud while Ezekial listened and nodded intently every so often. So far, nothing significant had happened amidst the pages. Thomas continued to court Isabel, and she seemed grateful for the attention and company. Isabel continued to write about how excited she was that he lavished her with gifts, which Emma found peculiar since the woman had inherited a mansion and could afford an expensive overseas trip and most likely anything else she wanted to buy. The three of them were still poring over the diary when the saloon door burst open and Thomas Benson's frame filled the entryway, flanked by two men who looked like they were trying to be tough but were failing miserably. They kept glancing out of the corners of their eyes at Thomas, as if they were waiting for direction from him. The wind slammed the saloon door shut, and one of the men visibly flinched.

Emma covered her smile with her hand as she saw Nancy let out a silent guffaw of laughter. The two women looked at each other, then looked away quickly as Thomas spoke.

"Jack!" Thomas barked out. "We're here to see you!"

"Well, no kidding," Nancy said under her breath. "Who else would you be here to see?"

Emma giggled nervously.

The two men followed Thomas to the bar where Nancy, Jack, Ezekial, and Emma were sitting. Emma noticed that Thomas's henchmen stood behind him, letting him do all the talking.

"I'm not sure what you're hoping to accomplish here," Jack said, staring Thomas directly in the face. "You said before that the taxes were in arrears. I still have thirty days to come up with the payment."

"Sure," scoffed Thomas. "Where are you going to get the money from? You don't even have any paying customers. This town is going nowhere, until I buy out everyone and demolish this place."

Emma hated to admit it, but Thomas was right. There were no paying customers. The current patrons of the bar were either its employees or people who were trading their goods and services for a meal and a drink. It didn't seem like there were more than twenty people in this town, and unless a big group happened to travel through in the next thirty days, the money was not exactly going to roll in. Looking at Nancy and Jack, she had a feeling they were thinking the exact same thing.

"Why are you so hellbent on taking over the saloon and the town?" Jack asked.

Thomas said nothing and looked over his shoulder, first at the man to his right and then at the man to his left. Neither one made eye contact with him.

"You're doing a terrible job of running this saloon, your father did a terrible job before you, and his father did a terrible job before him," he finally said, adjusting his cowboy hat.

Jack stared at Thomas. "I'm going to ask you kindly to leave my establishment."

"Or what?" sneered one of Thomas's buddies.

"Or I'm going to call Sheriff Campbell and ask him to forcefully remove you," Jack replied.

"Oh please. I'm not scared of him. I kicked his butt in grade school, and I have no problem doing it again," Thomas smirked.

"It's a little bit different now that you're adults and he's a man of the law," Jack replied solemnly.

"We'll see," Thomas said. He made a motion to his buddies, and all three of them turned and walked towards the door.

One of the men slammed the door shut with so much force that the whole building rattled, and Jack, Emma, Ezekial, and Nancy sat in stunned silence.

Finally, Nancy burst out laughing. "Talk about a grade school bully. 'I kicked his butt in grade school, and I have no problem doing it again,'" she mimicked. "I doubt he could pull off the same moves he had in grade school."

Jack broke out into a smile, and he and Emma started laughing at the absurdity of it all. Ezekial just sat there, bewildered.

Suddenly the saloon door opened, and everyone at the bar jumped in their seats.

"Whoa there," said the man at the entryway.

Jack stood up and ran to greet him. "Sheriff Campbell! Please come in." The two shook hands and walked towards the bar. "I'd like you to meet Emma. She's staying here with us for a while until we can get her stagecoach repaired."

"Well, I'll be," Sheriff Campbell said, removing his cowboy hat and taking Emma's outstretched hand. "Pleased to meet you."

Emma smiled at the man as he grasped her hand in a firm yet careful grip. His blue eyes looked right at her in that watchful way that a true man of the law often did out of habit. His smile was kind, and his tousled brown hair gave Emma the impression that he had been running his hands through his hair out of frustration.

The sheriff took a seat next to Jack, and Nancy got up and walked around the bar to pour him a drink. "You look like you could use this," she said, offering him a glass full of clear liquid. "Long day?"

Sheriff Campbell sighed. "Jack, I have to tell you something. I feel terrible about this," he said, then took a sip of his drink. He grimaced as he swallowed the drink, then gingerly took another sip.

Jack looked at him expectantly. "What is it? Do we need to go somewhere private?"

The sheriff took in his audience. "No, not unless you want to. I don't think this is news that anyone here can't know."

Nancy poured Jack a glass of the same clear liquid, and he took a sip. "Go on," he encouraged.

Sheriff Campbell took a deep breath. "I just passed Thomas and his buddies in the street, and I know what he's been up to. It feels like it's my fault that he caught on to the fact that your business owes some back taxes," he stopped, then took another sip of his drink.

Jack looked at him quizzically. "Okay, but technically isn't that stuff public record? Thomas could have looked that up any time he wanted. All he would have had to do was go to your office and request the records.

The sheriff sighed again. "Yeah, but I practically handed him those records."

Jack recoiled in his seat. "What?"

"Not on purpose!" Sheriff Campbell exclaimed. "I had paid Benson Enterprises a visit about something totally unrelated to you or the saloon. Thomas was actually trying to buy the vacant general store. As you know, the store has been out of operation for some time. The previous owners also owed some back taxes, and they just never could get out of debt. That wasn't what ended them of course. Their problem was they let too many people purchase things on credit and never collected payment. Anyway, I had the paperwork for the back taxes on the store in a manilla folder, and at the bottom of the pile was an old ledger from when your grandfather owned the saloon. Apparently, he hadn't paid taxes the first year or so the store was open. Thomas found that paperwork in the folder."

"Why was he going through your papers?" Nancy asked.

"I set the folder on the edge of the desk in front of me when we sat down to have a meeting at Benson Enterprises," the sheriff began. "We were talking about the general store, and I got sick suddenly. It might have been something I ate, but whatever it was, it hit me quickly.

I ran to the bathroom, and by the time I felt like I could walk back to the office, he'd gone through the entire contents of the folder. When I walked back in the room, he was holding the tax paperwork of your grandfather's in his hand."

"Wow," breathed Emma. She rolled these details around in her mind. Yes, the tax paperwork was public record. But the way Thomas found it seemed extremely suspicious. What had he really been looking for?

"Don't beat yourself up over it," Jack said. "Whether he found the paperwork in your folder or got ahold of the information some other way, he'd still try to do something corrupt."

Nancy nodded in agreement.

"Wait a minute," interjected Ezekial, who had been silent this whole time. "What did you eat that day you were in Thomas's office?"

"Well..." Sheriff Campbell sighed, looking off into the distance. "I have no idea what I ate that day. I most likely had the same thing to eat as I do most days. Something at my house in the morning for breakfast and then something here or at the inn for lunch. Why do you ask?"

Ezekial paused for a moment, seemingly gathering his thoughts. "This could be nothing," he said slowly. "But did you eat anything in his office?"

The sheriff perked up with a realization. "I did eat some chocolates that he offered me. They were imported from somewhere, I think he said. He offered me one as soon as I sat down at his desk. They were good, now that I remember it. Why do you ask?"

Ezekial ignored the question and instead, asked one of his own. "Did Thomas eat any of this chocolate?"

The sheriff took another swig of his drink, then set his glass down carefully. "I don't really remember," he said. "He offered me the candy and talked about what high quality it was. He said it was from Belgium or something and that it was expensive. He alluded to the fact that he had eaten a bunch of it when he first had it shipped here, but no, I can't remember if he ate any that day or not for sure."

Ezekial sat back on his barstool and rubbed the stubbly beard on his chin. "I just know Isabel talked an awful lot about those chocolates he used to bring her. I just wonder if there's any connection, that's all."

Everyone sat in stunned silence. Emma picked up the diary and flipped ahead to the next few entries. More flowers, a necklace, and sure enough, some Belgian chocolates, all gifted to Isabel by Thomas Benson. She pointed this out to the group.

"That doesn't necessarily mean the chocolates were poisoned though," Jack pointed out.

"True," said Emma as she continued to scan the diary. "Wait. Maybe it does. Listen to this: February 15th. Thomas visited me on Valentine's Day and brought me some beautiful flowers and a large box of imported chocolates. They tasted absolutely delicious, and before I knew it, I had gotten sick from eating so many."

Emma looked up from the diary and studied the faces of the rest of the group. They all wore expressions of skeptical shock. "It might be related. It's possible to eat so much chocolate that you become sick. Or it's possible the chocolate itself made her sick. We may never know."

Ezekial pulled a pencil out of his shirt pocket and made a note on the cover of the folder he had with him. "Well, if I had to guess, I would say this is connected somehow."

Everyone nodded in agreement.

The afternoon turned into evening, and one by one, the sheriff, Nancy, and Ezekial left the saloon and headed for home. Emma and Jack sat at the bar, sipping their drinks, and mulling over the events of the day.

"I can't believe he just charged in here," Emma said. "Unfortunately, it's us against him and he knows it."

Jack smiled when Emma said "us." He cleared his throat. "Does that mean you're willing to stay and help us fight him?"

Emma smiled, then blushed and looked down at her hands that were folded in her lap. "I guess I don't really have much choice, seeing as how I can't travel now, do I?"

Her stomach turned after she said the words. She hadn't meant to sound as if the only reason she was here was because she couldn't leave. Her broken stagecoach may have brought her here, but Emma realized she was in no hurry to get it repaired.

"I wouldn't mind if those stagecoach parts took a while to get here," Jack said quietly.

Emma's blush turned a darker shade of red. "I wouldn't either," she said.

The two sat in silence for a few seconds, until the wind knocked one of the window shutters against the wall of the saloon, snapping both of them back to reality.

"What are we going to do? We need to have some kind of defense for when Thomas returns. Because you know he'll be back," Emma said.

Jack nodded agreeably. "I'm not sure what he can really do though. We have thirty days to come up with the payment. Until then, I doubt we'll see him. He definitely won't be paying any money to come in for dinner or a drink."

Emma laughed nervously. "That's true. You know him and his buddies won't give you a dime to put towards the back taxes."

Jack looked out the window onto the dusty street. "Come on," he said. "I'll walk you to the inn."

***

The next morning, the same crew met at the saloon—Jack, Nancy, Ezekial, Emma, and Sheriff Campbell. They once again sat at the bar and began poring over the diary, but so far, the entries were still the same for the most part. Thomas Benson continued to court Isabel. He brought her flowers and chocolates and dresses and jewelry. Emma was reading one entry out loud when Sheriff Campbell grew noticeably withdrawn.

"Can you repeat that last one, please?" he asked.

Emma flipped back to the previous page. "The one from March first? Okay, here goes. Thomas visited today and brought me the most exquisite gemstone. It is blood red in color, and he said it was rare. He called it Rhodochrosite, but I had to ask him to repeat it at least three times."

Everyone turned to look at Sheriff Campbell, whose teeth were clenched so tightly that the muscle in his jaw was twitching.

"He stole that gem from me," the sheriff said quietly. "Of course, he gave it away. It meant nothing to him, but it's a rare gemstone." He grimaced.

Everyone waited for him to continue. He took a deep breath. "We were kids. Grade school, like eight years old or so. My mother passed shortly after she had my baby sister, but right before that, she gave me this gem. It was rare, and I'm not sure where she got it from. She gave it to me because she said if something happened to her, I would have to take care of my sister. She said red meant courage."

The silence in the saloon was deafening. Emma, Jack, Nancy, and Ezekial stared at Sheriff Campbell.

"Go on," Nancy said quietly, grabbing yesterday's bottle from the shelf, pouring the clear liquid into a glass, and sliding the glass across the bar.

The sheriff took a big breath. "Shortly after my mom died, I was walking home from school with my friend Eileen. I had been crying that morning, and Thomas came up behind me. He and his friends started laughing at me, the way grade school boys do. I reached into my pocket to hold onto the gem, but when Thomas punched me, I went sprawling to the ground and the stone flew out of my hand. I had minor injuries, just a scraped knee and a black eye. Eileen ran over to me to help me up, and Thomas grabbed the gem and ran. I don't even think he knew what it was. He just knew it was something I treasured."

"Oh my goodness. How awful," gushed Emma.

The others murmured their agreement.

"He probably didn't actually know it was worth anything." Sheriff Campbell shrugged. "Maybe he did."

The only sound in the saloon was the scratching of Ezekial's pencil making notes in his notebook.

Jack stood up angrily, startling everyone. "That's it!" he snorted. "If Thomas so much as walks past my door, there will be a problem."

"Hang on, Jack," Sheriff Campbell said. "He's not worth getting into trouble over."

Nancy looked at him and let out a lighthearted laugh. "You're the law, Sheriff."

No one could argue with that.

Nancy's lighthearted comment was soon overshadowed by dark clouds gathering in the distance. The wind picked up, and the limbs of the tree that sat behind the saloon could be heard scraping the metal roof of the building. Lightning flashed, and the lights flickered a few times.

Right on cue, the front door burst open and Thomas and his two buddies sauntered in.

"Howdy," he called out. "Hope we didn't break up your little party here. But we're on our way to pay a visit to the next town over, and it's about to rain. We thought we would camp out here until the storm blows over."

No one made eye contact. Emma looked in the mirror that hung behind the bar. In the reflection, she could see Thomas and his men standing there, seemingly waiting for a reaction from someone. Beside her, Sheriff Campbell was taking deep breaths. Thomas and his friends walked over to a table and made a show of removing their cowboy hats and then pulling out chairs to sit.

"Should I see if they want food?" Nancy whispered, looking at Jack.

"No!" hissed Sheriff Campbell. "We want them out of here as soon as possible." He straightened his tie, then looked sheepishly at Jack. "Sorry," he said quietly. "You do what you want, Jack. This is your establishment."

"He's right," Jack said, pointing to the sign behind the bar which read "Management Reserves the Right to Refuse Service to Unruly Customers."

Jack turned to Thomas and his friends, who were still sitting at the table, watching everyone. "I'm going to have to ask you all to leave."

"Oh now, come on," Thomas said, looking at his buddies and grinning. "We haven't been unruly yet."

"We both know why you're here," Jack said as he rose to his feet. "I will ask you one more time before I have to get the law involved. You and your friends need to leave the premises."

Tension filled the air. Thomas and his friends stared at Jack, Ezekial, Sheriff Campbell, Emma, and Nancy. The group stared back at them. Nancy slowly moved to the back of the bar, picked up a glass bottle, and poured the last remaining drops of its contents down the drain. She then gripped the bottle in one hand and stood positioned with her hand behind her back, narrowing her eyes. Ezekial removed his glasses and scooted his chair back from the bar. Emma looked around for something to use as a weapon and settled on a plate that held the remnants of her lunch. She moved the plate closer to her.

Without warning, Thomas and his buddies abruptly stood up from their chairs. His hand flew to his side and gripped the gun holster that hung from his belt. Sheriff Campbell removed his own gun and drew on the men in one swift motion. Nancy ran around to the front of the bar, wielding the glass bottle she had been holding. Emma stood up, knocking her barstool over in the process. Sheriff Campbell walked forward slowly, pointing his gun straight at Thomas.

When the sheriff started to cross the room, one of the men swiftly drew his pistol. Without thinking, Emma reflexively launched her plate at Thomas like a frisbee. In what seemed like slow motion, the plate sailed directly into his shoulder, knocking him backwards a few steps. The man next to him fired his pistol into the air. Ceiling particles and wood splinters rained to the floor as Nancy's startled scream pierced the air.

"You have thirty seconds to leave the property," Sheriff Campbell said through gritted teeth. "Starting. Now."

Thomas looked at the sheriff and the rest of the unlikely fighters, then let out a guffaw. "Or what? I kicked your butt when we were kids and I have no problem doing it again," he said.

"You were a bully then, and you're a bully now!" exclaimed Emma.

"You still have women fighting your battles for you?" Thomas sneered at Sheriff Campbell.

Sheriff Campbell charged forward, gun drawn. Two shots rang out, almost simultaneously. It was not entirely clear who had fired first. Somewhere behind her, Emma heard glass shattering. Nancy lurched forward, swinging the bottle and connecting with one of the henchmen's heads, who then slumped to the floor. Sheriff Campbell continued to move forward, steadily aiming his gun at Thomas. Emma looked over her shoulder to see where the damage was and saw the remnants of a bottle of liquor on the back of the bar, and shards of glass everywhere.

"Get out of this saloon and get out of this town," Sheriff Campbell said, still holding his gun steady.

"I own most of this town. In thirty days, I'll own even more of it," Thomas said.

"Not if I can help it," Sheriff Campbell replied.

Thomas rolled his eyes.

Ezekial and Jack moved forward, wielding barstools. Thomas cocked the hammer on his gun, and so did Sheriff Campbell. The man who was still standing took one look at Thomas and ran out the door of the saloon. Ezekial and Jack bombarded Thomas with barstools, just as he fired his weapon. Sheriff Campbell returned a shot, which grazed Thomas's arm. Everyone watched Thomas fall to the floor. A small puddle of blood began to seep through his shirt.

"Geez, Ethan," Thomas gasped, holding his shoulder. "I didn't know you had it in you."

Sheriff Campbell said nothing as he nudged the man on the floor with the toe of his boot. He trained his gun on Thomas, until he struggled to his feet and collected his scattered belongings, not saying a word as he limped out the door.

Chapter 5: In Search of the Heiress

The atmosphere in the saloon was tense for the rest of the day. Ezekial was a nervous wreck, checking the door every few minutes. Sheriff Campbell was wired, jumping out of his chair every few minutes to shout things like "I can't *believe* I let him get to those papers!" and "I hope my mother's ghost haunts him!" Every time Ezekial or Sheriff Campbell would have an outburst, Nancy would flinch. When Nancy stopped making jokes, Emma knew things were going downhill quickly for their makeshift sleuthing group.

Finally, Jack decided to close the saloon early. Nancy, Ezekial, and Sheriff Campbell left soon after, each claiming they had things to do. Once the sheriff left, after checking with Jack a minimum of three times to see if he was okay, Jack flipped the sign on the door to read Closed. He turned around and looked at Emma, who was not sure if she should go back to the inn or stay here.

He made his way back to the bar and sat down next to her. "Are you up for reading some more of the diary? I don't think I'm ready to go home just yet, and I know I won't be able to sleep."

Emma nodded. "I was thinking the same thing. Surely there is more to this diary than page upon page of Thomas bringing her gifts all the time. That would be boring to even the loneliest of women I think."

Jack smiled. "I knew I liked you."

Emma blushed as she opened the diary back up and set it on the bar between them.

"Okay, let's see," she said, keeping her eyes focused on the pages in the hopes that by avoiding eye contact with Jack, she could prevent her blush from deepening. She located the last entry they had read.

"Here we go. April 2nd. The rains have kept Thomas away for a few days, as the roads flood quickly, so I am back to being at home by myself. I have been spending most of my time in the library on the third floor, watching the clouds roll in. I feel safer up here because every time the thunder rolls, the whole house rattles. Yesterday I would have sworn that someone was trying to unlatch the cellar door. Darcy heard it too and went scurrying under the sofa, letting out one fierce sounding 'meow!' I definitely couldn't leave her up here all alone after that."

Emma stopped reading. "Do you think that's anything? That she thought it sounded like someone was breaking in?"

Jack frowned. "No, I don't think so. Maybe she was just saying that the thunder was so loud that she and the cat were freaked out."

Emma pursed her lips. "Possibly. Let's keep reading. Okay, where was I? April 3rd. The rain finally broke today, and I went outside just to walk around the yard. I'm lucky to have no storm damage high on this hill, and it's likely to be a day or two before the water in the creek will go down enough for Thomas to be able to cross. While I was walking around the yard, I saw that the cellar hatch had flown open in the wind. I guess Darcy had every right to be scared after all."

Emma looked up at Jack. "How likely do you think it is that the cellar door just burst open like that?"

Jack shrugged. "It could happen. The Monroe mansion is one of the oldest houses in town. If Isabel had been living there by herself for a while, it might not be in great shape."

Emma wasn't entirely convinced, but Jack could be right. She kept reading.

"April fourth. I've been getting restless now that I've gotten used to having company again. I walked around outside for a while today. The cellar hatch was blown open for the second day in a row. I started to go down the stairs but thought better of it and scurried right back up into the daylight. There might be animals down there, maybe rats or something bigger, like possums. Hopefully the water will have drained down soon, at least far enough that Thomas will be able to get across the creek. I'll ask him to check the cellar and secure the door. Even though animals can't get into the house from the cellar, it's still troublesome to know that something is crawling around right underneath where I am."

Emma looked at Jack again. "What are the odds that the hatch would blow open two days in a row?"

Jack raised his shoulders in a more exaggerated shrug this time. He looked skeptical. "Maybe?"

Emma was baffled but continued reading. "April fifth. I strolled the grounds restlessly today, waiting for Thomas. I peered around the corner, terrified that the cellar hatch would be blown open again. What a relief I felt when I saw that the hatch was closed. The lock had come unfastened, so I scurried over, refastened the lock, and then to my surprise, Thomas was right behind me! He came to surprise me with flowers and chocolates after our days apart."

Emma closed the diary and looked at Jack. "Still think that hatch blew open from the wind?"

"Absolutely not. Want to go see the mansion?" he asked, scratching his chin.

Emma's heart fluttered and her eyes grew wide. "Of course! That's music to my investigative journalist ears!"

Jack smiled. "Let's go then. If we start walking now, we can at least see the house and the grounds before it gets too dark."

Emma was elated. Not only was she going to see the mysterious home where the elusive Isabel lived, but she was also going to get to spend more time with Jack, just the two of them. She followed him to the door, then felt her skin tingle as he briefly placed his hand on her lower back to escort her out the door. They began walking down the dusty, deserted street. The sidewalks were cracked, and Emma grabbed Jack's arm as the toe of her boot caught on an uneven block of pavement. He held her arm to steady her as they walked down the only street in town. As Jack pointed out the abandoned storefronts and recalled what they previously were, Emma felt a sadness wash over her as she saw what the town had been and still could be.

Finally, they reached the edge of town and began their ascension up the steep hill towards the very house that Emma had noticed from a distance when she was in her stagecoach. As they crossed the wooden bridge, Jack pointed out the creek, now safely in its banks, that Isabel had spoken of in her diary. Emma could see how a little rain might be detrimental to the tiny creek and anything that was near its narrow banks.

Finally, they reached the top of the hill. Emma took in her surroundings and let out a sigh. The three-story rambling mansion was beautiful, although its white clapboard was weathered. Like every other building in town, the paint was peeling, and several shutters were missing. However, the house was one of a kind and Emma couldn't help but notice its grandeur. Every window in the front had window boxes, although there were now weeds growing out of them. The wrap-around front porch was framed at the top by scalloped, intricate woodwork.

"Wow," Emma breathed. "It's gorgeous."

"I know," Jack agreed. "It's a shame that the house has gone downhill. Isabel's parents died tragically when she was sixteen. She was an only child, and so inherited the family property by default. But it was too much for anyone to keep up by themselves, much less a young girl. Her grandmother came to live with her for a while, but then she passed also, and Isabel was left alone again."

"How tragic," Emma said quietly.

Jack nodded his head. "Yes. So, when she disappeared, I think it really took the town by surprise. Everyone knew she had a hard time. Who would kidnap her, or worse, and why?"

Emma shook her head. "I can't even imagine."

They stood on the edge of the worn trail, looking at the mansion. The sun was starting to set, casting long shadows on the lawn. The long chain that held the light above the front door swayed slightly in the wind, giving the house an eerie look.

Jack looked at Emma. "Are you ready?"

Emma grimaced. "As ready as I'm going to be, I guess. It's different now that we're here in person." she giggled nervously.

"Let's just look around, and if you decide at any time you want to leave, just say the word, and we can go," Jack said.

She took a deep breath. "Okay. I think I'm ready then."

They walked over to the house. Jack placed one foot on the bottom stair, testing his weight. He climbed the steps, then stopped to look down at Emma, who then gingerly climbed the steps and stood next to Jack as he examined the front door.

"Do you think we need a key?" Emma whispered.

"I'm not sure," Jack said, trying the doorknob, which turned easily. He gave the door one swift push, and it swung open with ease. The two peeked into the abandoned house and were met with a stale, mildewy smell. Jack stepped over the threshold and held his hand back for Emma. She took his hand and stepped through the doorway, once again overtaken by the grandeur of the house. The foyer had a gorgeous crystal chandelier suspended from a high ceiling and mirrors on every side to magnify the lighting. In the afternoon sunlight, prisms reflected on the mirrors. A round mahogany table holding a crystal vase stood in the middle of the room. The vase, once shiny and filled with flowers, held only dust and dried leaves now. The remnants of the flowers were scattered on the table and floor. Jack tiptoed through the foyer and motioned for Emma to follow.

They walked through the house, inspecting each of the rooms. There was a grand piano and fluffy couch in a sitting room, a beautiful mahogany table with enough chairs for a large dinner party in the formal dining room, and a massive kitchen and summer pantry. Every room had a fireplace, large windows, and an intricate color scheme with wallpaper and drapes to match. Everything was covered in a layer of dust. Several of the rooms had water spots on the walls and bubbling plaster where water had seeped through. Jack and Emma were making their way to the second floor when Jack stopped suddenly.

"What is it?" Emma asked, her heart in her throat. Had someone followed them up here? Was the house not really abandoned?

"The cellar," Jack said, stopping on the second stair and turning around to descend. "We should check out the hatch doors before it gets too dark."

Emma had completely forgotten about the cellar once they got up the hill and she had seen the house and told Jack as much.

The two made their way back outside, then slowly crept behind the house. The hatch to the cellar was still intact, although Jack had to clear a plethora of weeds and overgrown grass from around the opening to get a good look at the doors. He tossed the unwanted greenery over his shoulder, then bent to look at the latch.

"What is it?" Emma asked, noticing his frown.

"I can't figure out how this thing could have come open, no matter how windy it was. The first day, maybe, if the latch wasn't fastened. But once she closed it, it should have stayed shut."

Jack pointed to the slide mechanism. He was right. The latch was metal, and one piece of the latch had to slide into the other piece, then the top piece was pushed down into a little groove to keep it in place. It was highly improbable that the wind lifted the top latch, slid it over, and blew open the doors.

"I don't think that's something an animal could figure out either," said Emma. She looked around the abandoned property and shuddered.

Jack nodded slowly. "Yeah. I agree. I think it was a person."

Emma nodded her head in agreement as a chill went through her spine. "Do you think someone is still down there? Or that they'll come back?"

Jack looked around at the abandoned property, then up to the third story of the house. "I don't think so. I think whatever they were after was something to do with Isabel. And even if they do plan to return, the odds of them coming back when we're here are pretty slim. They clearly haven't been down in the cellar for quite some time."

Emma felt a little better hearing this. She took a deep breath and wiped her sweaty palms on her dress. "True. But still, it seems so creepy. Surely Isabel would have realized that it wasn't the wind?"

Jack looked at her for a second, then looked back at the latch. "Unless the latch was changed. It looks like this could be newer, or at least newer than the rest of the house."

Emma's eyes widened as she realized what this could mean.

Jack gingerly unhooked the latch, then lifted one of the doors, then the other one. They were old and heavy, their green paint long faded. The afternoon sun shone just bright enough to illuminate the stairs that descended into the cellar.

"Shall we?" he asked, standing on the top step.

Emma faltered. She wasn't sure she wanted to go into the cellar, but she certainly didn't want to stand outside by herself either. She began to descend the stairs behind Jack. It took her eyes a few seconds to adjust to the dim lighting once they were in the cellar. Upon first glance, there didn't seem to be anything of interest. Garden tools and an old broom stood in the corner, leaning against some shelves. Two or three cans stood on each shelf, the vegetables floating in their own juices. Jack looked around the cellar, disappointment obvious in his features.

"Who would come down here for this?" he asked.

"Either they were hiding from something down here," Emma said, "or they were doing the hiding of something."

Jack nodded his head slowly. "You could be right."

He ducked his head and continued farther into the basement, rubbing his hands along the walls to check, but for what, Emma was not sure. Suddenly, he let out a startled sound.

"Emma!" he called excitedly. "I think I've found something!"

As she made her way over to him, he grabbed her hand, placing it on the wall.

"Feel that?" he asked.

Emma wasn't sure if she was feeling the same thing he was. The dirt did seem a little softer in the spot, like this part of the cellar was dug out and lightly packed back in.

"The soil? It does seem to be a little different here," she remarked.

Jack nodded excitedly. "I think so too. There's got to be something behind there."

Jack looked around the cellar frantically, then grabbed a small garden trowel. He started chipping away at the dirt, until an entire section crumbled. There, stuck haphazardly in the wall, was a wooden box, about the size of a hat box, but square in diameter.

Jack dropped the trowel, then grabbed Emma's hand once again. "I think we found something! Should we take it out?"

Emma had visions of ghosts and evil spirits escaping once the box was open, but she couldn't resist the temptation to know what was in there. She nodded her head, then braced herself to dart back up the stairs and out into the open air. Jack painstakingly pulled the box out of the place where it was wedged into the wall. He placed it on the cellar floor in front of them, then looked at Emma and said, "Maybe we should open it outside, where we can see?"

She looked at the box, then back at him. "Yes. Come on!"

She darted up the stairs, Jack at her heels. He placed the box on the ground in the tall grass, and they crouched down side by side.

"Ready?" he asked.

Emma took a deep breath, then nodded. "Okay," she said.

Jack slowly lifted the lid of the box. Emma flinched, then giggled nervously.

In the bottom of the box was a gold coin and a single key. Jack and Emma looked at each other. He reached in to pick up the coin, rubbing his fingers and thumb across the top and bottom of it, staring off into the distance.

"Why would someone hide a single gold coin in here?" Emma asked. "Do you think there's more where this came from?"

Jack looked at the coin. "My guess is that this key will take us to the rest of the coins. I bet there are more boxes hidden around the property with different coins and keys that would lead us to their hiding spot, if the boxes are still here."

Emma shuddered, then looked up at the huge house. The sun was just beginning to set, casting long shadows across the lawn. She didn't know if she was up for going back inside the mansion in the dark, even if Jack was with her, and was really hoping he wouldn't suggest it.

"I think we should take this box to Ezekial. He knows everything about this town, going back to when it was founded. If there really is a buried treasure, he would know," Jack said.

"Do you think it's Isabel's treasure, or do you think someone was sneaking in the cellar to hide it here?" Emma asked.

Jack shook his head. "I'm not sure, but if I had to guess, someone was sneaking in there for some reason."

He closed the lid on the box and stood up. Emma followed his lead. They closed the cellar doors in silence. Jack tucked the wooden box under one arm, then offered his other hand to Emma. She gratefully took his hand, and the two walked back into town, speculating where the treasure could be, if it still existed, or if it could have something to do with Isabel's disappearance.

Jack walked Emma to the front door of the inn, and after giving her a small kiss on the cheek, they agreed to meet early the next morning to piece together more of the clues. She darted up the stairs, her hand over her cheek where he had kissed her. She tossed and turned all night, thinking of Jack's kiss and the hidden box they had found together.

Finally, just as the sun was starting to rise, Emma gave up on getting a good night's sleep and got up, dressing carefully in the dim light. She chose a dress that elongated her neckline and made her look graceful, complementing her fair skin and blonde hair. When she went down to the dining room, Jack and Sarah were already sitting at a table. Sarah jumped up to give her a motherly hug.

"Oh, sweet girl," Sarah said, wrapping her arms around Emma's slim frame.

"I filled Sarah in on everything that happened yesterday," Jack said.

"I'm so sorry you've gotten involved in all of this," Sarah said. "The town has a lot of hidden secrets, some of which are very dark, I'm afraid."

Emma smiled. "It's okay, really. This is what I want to do. Investigative journalism. If nothing else, this is great practice for my next job." She didn't add that maybe she wouldn't mind staying here, in this town with Nancy and Sarah and Ezekial and Sheriff Campbell, and most of all, Jack.

Just then the front door opened, and several seconds later, Ezekial appeared in the doorway of the dining room.

"I hope it's okay that I join you," he said, looking around from Sarah, to Jack, to Emma.

"Of course!" Sarah exclaimed, crossing the room to get another table setting from the cupboard. "You know you're always welcome here."

Ezekial smiled and took a seat. "You all looked so serious when I came in, I was afraid that I was interrupting something."

"Well, we do have a story for you," Jack began.

Ezekial poured himself some coffee and looked at Jack, then at Emma. "Does this have anything to do with the walk I saw you two taking yesterday?"

The two looked sheepishly at each other. "Yes," they said in unison.

Ezekial chuckled. "I thought so. I saw you walking back through town, right about dusk. I would know that wooden box you were carrying anywhere."

Emma and Jack looked at each other quizzically.

Ezekial continued. "Isabel was engaged to a man named Dakota, long ago, who died tragically in a freak accident. But his family had money, or at least gold. All those wooden boxes were carved on the Indian reservation. His family was Native American, you know."

Emma nodded slowly. "So, there are more of these boxes?" she asked.

Ezekial nodded his head vigorously. "Oh, yes. I would say quite a few more. When Dakota and Isabel got engaged, he showed her where the boxes were. Isabel brought them to me to verify the authenticity of the gold. Of course, when Dakota died, his will specified that she inherit the money. I have no idea if she kept the boxes at her house or in a hidden spot somewhere."

Jack told Ezekial about the diary entries that led them to look at the old house, the cellar doors that could not have been opened by the wind, and the weird hole dug in the basement wall that housed the box. He opened the box and showed Ezekial the key and the single gold coin.

Ezekial frowned. "Let me see that key," he said, reaching across the table.

Jack handed it to him, and Ezekial turned the key over in his hand a few times. It was dirty, and he scraped some dirt off with his fingernail. He let out a gasp, and positioned his thumb and forefinger around an initial that was engraved on the key: the letter B.

"B! The letter B!" Ezekial exclaimed, looking around the room.

The occupants of the table stared at him quizzically.

"B for Benson?" Ezekial mused. "I don't know this for sure, and obviously this is just speculation. But Thomas Benson was acting really weird after Dakota died. He was out of town when the accident happened, but he came into town for the funeral. He was standing outside the graveyard, just watching the procession. It was creepy."

"Everything about him seems creepy," Emma chimed in. "And I barely know him."

Chapter 6: Love Triangle

Emma and Jack were sitting in the saloon, telling Nancy and Sheriff Campbell about their impromptu treasure hunt and the latest diary entry, when they all heard the unmistakable clopping of horse hooves on the street outside. Emma turned to the window curiously, knowing she would most likely not know who was coming into town anyway. A woman sat on top of the horse, her perfect posture and calm demeanor looking like something from an advertisement. Her dark hair was long and loose, and looked as if she had just brushed it despite the fact that she had been riding a horse through the windy town. The woman dismounted from the horse in one swift motion and smoothed her skirt with her delicate hands. Her small frame was curvy, and her dark lowcut dress accentuated her curves. Emma looked down at her own plain dress and checked her reflection in the mirror. The pastel-colored dress that she had put on this morning suddenly looked childish compared to this glamorous stranger. She glanced sideways at Jack. His eyes were fixed on the woman. Her stomach dropped.

The door opened, and the woman floated through. She paused in the doorway, and Jack rushed to greet her.

"Who is that?" Emma whispered to Nancy.

"Charlotte Rose," Nancy whispered back. "Dakota's sister. I haven't seen her since the funeral."

Emma nodded.

Jack made a show of helping Charlotte Rose take a seat at the table, and he rushed to get her a water. Emma looked at Nancy, who was also watching him skeptically. Charlotte Rose took a long sip of water, set her glass down, and turned to the girls sitting at the bar.

"Hello," she cooed. "I'm Charlotte Rose." She extended an arm, clearly waiting for Emma to get up to come to her. She stood, shook the dainty hand, and introduced herself.

"It's great to see you again, Charlotte Rose," Nancy said.

"You as well," Charlotte Rose said.

An awkward silence descended on the room. Emma wondered what this woman wanted and how her presence was going to affect their detective work so far.

"I haven't heard from Isabel in quite some time, and I fear she is in grave danger," Charlotte Rose said, looking from Nancy to Jack to Emma.

The three of them looked at each other, and finally Jack spoke. "When is the last time you heard from Isabel?"

Charlotte Rose tilted her head. "I guess it's been a few months now. She and I kept in touch after Dakota died. But in her last letter, she mentioned that Thomas Benson had started calling on her, and I wrote back to tell her that he was bad news. I'm not sure if she never received my letter, if she was ignoring my advice, or if, God forbid, something has happened to her. That man is foul."

Nancy and Emma were silent. Jack cleared his throat. "Well, actually, Isabel is missing."

Charlotte Rose let out a gasp and fainted, falling to the floor. Jack rushed forward to catch her, just as her head was about to hit the ground. He splashed some water on her face, and she came to, apologizing profusely. "Oh goodness, I'm so embarrassed," she kept saying, over and over.

Emma sat quietly as she watched Jack tend to Charlotte Rose. Finally, when things calmed down, the group filled her in on the story of the diary and the missing treasure.

"I don't even know what to say," Charlotte Rose remarked. "I knew Dakota had three boxes of gold coins, because I had three boxes that were identical to his. If Thomas got his hands on the gold, the question is how?"

Jack, Emma, and Nancy nodded their heads in agreement. "I didn't know Isabel, of course," Emma said. "But do you think she would have told Thomas about the gold?"

"I'm not sure," Charlotte said slowly. "I don't really think so. She was so loyal to Dakota. If anything, she probably wanted to keep the gold for sentimental reasons. She definitely didn't need the money."

"Should we go back to the house today, in the daylight?" Jack asked.

The three ladies and Jack looked at each other. Emma and Charlotte nodded their heads. Nancy let out a little giggle. "Well, someone has to keep the saloon open and running for all these customers," she said.

"Is that a no from you?" Emma asked teasingly.

"That is an absolute no," Nancy said.

"Well, it's decided then. Are you sure?" Jack asked, looking at Nancy.

Nancy nodded her head vigorously.

"Okay, let's go," Jack said, already heading toward the door. Emma and Charlotte followed. Jack held the door open for Charlotte and followed out behind her, but Emma was a few paces behind, and she had to catch the door before it swung closed on her. She looked over her shoulder at Nancy, who was staring at her with wide eyes. Emma raised her eyebrows and followed Jack and Charlotte out the door.

The three of them began the same walk that Jack and Emma had taken less than forty-eight hours before. Emma walked quietly beside Jack and Charlotte as the two of them caught up since they had last seen each other. From what Emma could glean from the conversation, Charlotte had grown up in a town close to here, but often passed through on her way to visit friends or relatives in other states. The last time Charlotte had visited was for her brother Dakota's funeral, which had been several years ago.

The walk was agonizing to Emma. As Charlotte droned on, catching Jack up on her adventures, Emma found herself wishing she had just said something to Jack to even hint at her feelings. True, she had felt an intense connection and attraction to Jack from the very first day, but she had tried to stamp those feelings down because she assumed she would only be stopping for the evening and then heading on her way. As the days wore on and she spent more and more time with Jack, she became enamored with his easygoing personality and his rugged charm. Emma hoped it wasn't too late. Were Jack and Charlotte simply just catching up, or was there something more there?

Finally, they reached the top of the hill. The house loomed in front of them, like an intimidating giant. Jack once again tested the rickety front steps, then motioned for the girls to follow him inside. Even though Emma had seen the entryway and the sparkling chandelier just a day ago, she was still taken aback by the beauty of the home. The three of them toured through the main level of the house, then ascended the stairs. Large bedrooms made up the second floor, each with their own bathroom and clawfoot bathtub. Flowered wallpaper lined the walls, although the paper was peeling in several corners and the flowers were faded from so much sun exposure. They toured through each room, opening doors of chifforobes and drawers of desks and dressers. There seemed to be nothing of importance and no clues. Clothes still hung in the chifforobes, and each medicine cabinet had empty bottles of dried-up tinctures and lotions. Finally, Emma suggested going to the third floor, since that was where Isabel had written about spending most of her time.

Jack, Charlotte, and Emma went back to the main staircase and climbed the stairs to the third floor, which opened into a vast room with windows that overlooked the town on three sides. The fourth side was entirely wall-to-wall bookshelves. A desk and a couch sat in the center of the room. The table next to the couch still had a cup and saucer sitting on it. There was an open book laying facedown on the couch. Emma shuddered as she realized it was almost like Isabel could come walking back up the steps any minute and pick up where she left off in her book like nothing happened.

"I don't know what I expected to find," Jack said. "But I don't see anything that could point us in the right direction of Isabel or the missing treasure."

Emma and Charlotte nodded their heads in agreement.

"Do you think it would be wise to focus our efforts on Thomas Benson Enterprises?" Charlotte asked.

Jack stood looking out the window, contemplating. "If he does know something about Isabel's disappearance or the missing gold, he won't tell us. So, I'm not sure what we could gain from that."

"Did Thomas even show any bit of remorse or sadness when Isabel disappeared?" Charlotte asked.

Jack thought about it. "Not really. He was out of town when she disappeared, and he came back a few days after she was gone. I'm not sure anyone thought to ask him how he was doing, as we were all just focused on the fact that she was missing."

Charlotte nodded slowly and thoughtfully. "I say we head back down and read some more of the diary to find out what happened to Isabel the last few days before she disappeared."

Emma and Jack agreed, and the three of them made their way down the two flights of stairs and out the front door. Before they headed back down the hill and into town, Jack and Emma showed Charlotte the cellar and the hiding spot where they had found the wooden box.

"Wow," breathed Charlotte as she ran her hand over the dirt walls and the hole that had been dug. "I don't think this is a place where Dakota would have put the box, simply because he would have kept to Indian traditions, which would not have allowed him to bury the box inside a house, whether it was his fiancé's house or not."

Jack and Emma looked at each other. "So, you don't think that Isabel even knew this was here?" Emma asked.

Charlotte shook her head. "I don't think so, especially since she wrote in her diary that she heard the hatch doors opening. It seems like too much of a coincidence to me. Plus, she lived here by herself.

There were plenty of hiding places she could have used in the house that would not require her to go down to that creepy cellar. I don't think she was keeping the gold to cash in for money. I think she was keeping it for sentimental reasons and therefore wouldn't have hidden it in a dark cellar where she could never see it."

Emma had to agree.

The three of them closed the cellar hatches and made their way back to town, Charlotte and Jack still catching up, and Emma trailing along behind them, interjecting when Charlotte or Jack asked her a question. The whole afternoon left Emma exhausted, and when they got back into town, she told them she was going to her room to take a nap.

Emma opened the front door of the inn, relief flooding over her. She had just placed her foot on the bottom stair, looking forward to her big comfy bed, when Sarah passed through, seemingly on her way to the parlor, with a plate of cookies in her hand.

"Emma!" she exclaimed. "I didn't expect to see you until dinner. How did this afternoon go? Have you found out any more information?"

Emma sighed. As much as she wanted a nap, she welcomed the opportunity to see Sariah and tell her about the day, the visit to the house, and more importantly, the sudden appearance of Charlotte Rose. She turned around and followed Sarah to the parlor, where she began to recount her day's events. Sarah listened, grabbing a cookie off the plate every so often and either eating it herself or offering it to Emma. Emma accepted each cookie gratefully, and by the time the tray was empty, she had told Sarah about all the day's events, her feelings about Jack, and her worry about Charlotte coming in to steal Jack away from her.

"I can't even really say she's stealing Jack," Emma said tearfully. "I don't even know how Jack feels about me. I thought we both had this attraction towards each other, but now I wonder if it's all in my head.

Maybe Jack isn't taking me seriously because he thinks I'm just passing through."

"But are you just passing through?" Sarah said kindly. "You've been here a short amount of time, and you already fit right in with all of us. You've been great at helping us piece together clues about Isabel. Maybe it's time you think about staying here, at least for a little while."

A single tear dropped from Emma's eye, and she swiped at it, smiling in embarrassment. "I'm sorry," she said. "I don't know what came over me. Charlotte coming into town really shook things up. I can't compete with someone like that."

Sarah pulled a handkerchief from her pocket and handed it to Emma. "I don't think there's any competition going on here. Charlotte breezes through here every so often. She's a good person deep down, but has a lot of issues from losing her parents at a young age. She craves the attention she gets when she comes into town unexpectedly, but then gets bored quickly and moves on. She has the money and the connections to go wherever she wants."

Emma nodded her head, wondering if Sarah was hinting at the idea that if Charlotte could go anywhere, she wouldn't choose to stay in a little ghost town with less than twenty inhabitants.

Emma smiled. "Thank you, Sarah. I think I just need a nap. I'll be down for supper, hopefully feeling like a new person."

Sarah got up and gave Emma a motherly hug. "Don't you worry. Everything will be okay."

Emma trudged up the stairs and lay down on her bed. It wasn't long before she fell asleep. She had no idea how long she slept, but she woke up with a start when she realized she was almost late for dinner. She freshened her hair and makeup and made her way down the stairs. She was just rounding the corner to go into the dining room when she heard Jack's voice, and stopped short. She stood just outside the dining room doorway, leaning forward and listening for the response of whoever he was talking to. The end of what Jack had been saying sounded like "I can't believe she's back."

Emma's heart thudded in her chest and blood pounded in her ears so loud that she was afraid she wouldn't be able to hear the whole conversation. Sarah's voice came next.

"Yes, I can't either."

"I haven't seen her in years. She looks like a completely changed person. I can tell she was really attracted to me," Jack said.

"I'm sure she was," Sarah responded. "You know how she is. She comes into town, gets the attention she wants, and then leaves again. I'm not saying that to make her sound bad. But we all know she's had some issues since her parents died. It was a critical point in a young girl's life, and she missed the attention and nurturing that she needed. "

The room was silent, and Emma could picture Jack pondering Sarah's advice.

"Yes," agreed Jack. "But what if it's different this time? I just felt this intense attraction to her."

"Only you can decide how you truly feel," Sarah said. "But you can't lead both women on at the same time. I think you need to decide what you really want."

It was silent, and Emma stood at the doorway for a few seconds, wondering whether she should go into the dining room now or keep standing there. The front door of the inn opened, and Charlotte came down the hallway, heading towards the dining room.

"Good evening," she sang out, reaching out to touch Emma's arm as she walked by.

Emma followed her into the dining room, where Jack and Sarah sat. Dinner was served, and Emma ate quietly, watching Charlotte as she delicately cut her food into bite size pieces and made savory faces with every bite. Jack, seemingly unaware that anything was amiss, kept up his hearty banter like usual.

The next few days passed without any significance. Nancy, Ezekial, Jack, Emma, and Charlotte continued to read the diary entries and try to make any connections between Isabel, the missing treasure, and Thomas Benson. Emma found herself becoming increasingly short with Charlotte, who seemed to enjoy knowing she was causing a stir. After a long afternoon of listening to Charlotte talk about how she had gifted much of the silverware and glasses to the saloon when Jack had first taken over from his father, Emma decided she'd had enough.

She went back to the inn that evening and began packing her trunk. She wasn't sure how she was going to get all her belongings to her new destination, but she could ride Cinnamon and have this trunk shipped with whatever she could fit inside. The old, broken-down stagecoach could stay in this town with all the other old, broken-down buildings. Emma skipped dinner that evening and was putting the last of her dresses into the trunk when there came a knock at the door.

Emma opened it, and on the other side stood Jack, holding a bouquet of flowers he had clearly picked from outside.

"Before you say anything, I know it's not appropriate that I'm up here," he began. "I missed you at dinner. Sarah told me you were packing to leave, and I came up here to ask you to reconsider. Please give me a chance. I really don't want Charlotte and her flightiness. She will be a good asset to have while we try to find Isabel and the treasure, but she would not be a good partner. I'm sorry I made you feel less than. I realized I have feelings for you, feelings that are much stronger than anything I thought I had for Charlotte."

Emma dropped the dress from her hand and threw both arms around Jack's neck, embracing him as her heart swelled with relief and joy.

Chapter 7: Diary Revelations

The next morning, Jack and Emma sat at breakfast, poring over the diary again.

"I just feel like we're missing something," Emma said. "She keeps talking about Thomas and how he's bringing her all these gifts." She wound a strand of blonde hair around her fingers and looked across the table at Jack. He stared back at her, eyes twinkling, despite the grim circumstances of what they were reading.

"Okay, here we go," Emma continued. "May second. Thomas paid me a visit today, and I was taken completely by surprise. I was up in the library and hadn't heard him knock on the door. I had one of the boxes out that Dakota had given me and was sitting at the desk. When I saw Thomas come into the room, I slammed the box shut and tried to stuff it into the bottom drawer of the desk. I don't think he saw what I was doing, as he was facing the desk and couldn't see the drawers when he walked into the room, but he had a peculiar look on his face when the gold coins clanked together as the drawer slammed. He didn't say anything, just presented me with a beautiful bouquet of flowers as usual."

Emma stopped reading and looked at Jack, her eyes wide. "The gold was in the desk. Even if Thomas didn't know about it before, he might have suspected something then. A shady man like him would probably be able to pick out the sounds of money."

Jack nodded. "But that doesn't explain why she heard noises in the cellar before this."

Emma paused for a moment, "True. Unless he knew about some of the boxes, but not all of them."

Jack nodded slowly. "That could be. Let's keep reading."

"May third. I woke up this morning with a terrible headache. When Thomas came yesterday, he brought me chocolates. I'm sure that too much sugar consumption is causing these headaches. I must have slept for twelve hours last night." Emma stopped reading and looked at Jack. "Do you think there's a connection here? Every time she eats the chocolate he brings, she either gets sick or sleeps for a long time."

"How can we prove that?" Jack asked.

"And why doesn't she see the connection?" Emma asked.

"Yeah, but it's easier to see it from the outside looking in. She was definitely looking at him through rose-colored glasses. That, or she didn't *want* to see it," said Jack.

Emma kept reading. "I woke up, completely in a daze. I don't know why, but something made me open the desk drawer to make sure the gold was still there. Maybe it was a dream that I had. Either way, I opened the drawer and saw that the box was nestled safely in the bottom, so I laid back down and went to sleep some more. The sun was streaming in, and I felt so relaxed, stretching out on the couch, basking in the beams of light."

Emma stopped reading again. "Do you think the gold was still in the box? What if she just opened the desk drawer, saw the wooden box, and then just closed the drawer? What if the gold was already missing then?"

Jack looked at Emma as if he didn't know what to say. The two sat looking at each other in silence, deep in thought.

"Maybe we need to consult Ezekial," Jack suggested. "He probably has some insight on the gold and the boxes it was stored in."

Emma finished the last few bites of breakfast and pushed her plate back. She gathered the diary and followed Jack out the door. They walked up the street and made a few turns, onto an even dustier and more abandoned looking road, which had houses with peeling paint, missing shutters, and weeds overtaking the yards. Jack stopped in the middle of the block, placing his hand on the small of Emma's back to escort her up the sloping sidewalk to a white clapboard house with a sagging front porch.

They walked onto the front porch and knocked with the brass door knocker. Several seconds later, they heard a shuffling, and the curtains covering the front window parted. Ezekial's face peeked out skeptically, and he broke into a smile when he recognized Jack and Emma. He opened the door, gesturing for the pair to come inside.

"Hello, hello," he said, closing the door behind them and rushing to the sofa to clear off some papers so that his visitors would have a place to sit.

Emma sat on the edge of the sofa and looked around the room in awe. Every spare inch of the wall was covered in some form of memorabilia, from wanted posters to framed newspaper clippings. One entire wall had floor-to-ceiling bookcases, each stuffed tightly with books. Ezekial caught Emma looking around and gave a sheepish grin.

"Excuse the mess," he said. "I have memorabilia dating back to the founding of this town."

"It's impressive," she said, still gazing around.

"That's actually why we're here," Jack said. "Do you remember anything about the gold coins that Isabel inherited? Or the boxes that Dakota would have put them in?"

Ezekial pursed his lips in thought, then crossed the room to a desk that was also covered in newspapers.

"Yes," he said over his shoulder. "There's supposed to be a whole treasure hidden somewhere from the tribe of which Dakota and Charlotte were members. If you ask me, I think there's some truth to it."

He ruffled through a stack of papers, then came up with another diary-looking book, this one leatherbound and homemade-looking. It had ribbon dangling from the bottom, marking the spot in what Emma hoped was going to lead them closer to another clue.

Ezekial opened the book, then read a few sentences under his breath. Jack and Emma looked at him expectantly. "According to this, which I actually got from a distant ancestor of Dakota's, the boxes were carved specifically to house the gold coins. The authenticity can be verified by a carving on the top lid and initials on the bottom."

He brought the book over to Jack and Emma to show them a rough sketch of the boxes. Emma studied the drawing, then opened the diary. She flipped through the pages, skimming for any reference to the boxes or their authenticity.

"Hmmm," she mused, poring over the section they had just read. "I don't see any mention so far of these specific boxes, but she does mention having the box in a desk drawer and being afraid that Thomas would have heard the coins clanking together. I guess we should keep reading?" she glanced at Jack and Ezekial, who nodded vigorously.

"May sixth. The weather has been beautiful, with such nice sunny, spring days, so Thomas has been over to visit more frequently. We have been taking long walks in the garden. All the fresh air and sunshine has been making me sleepy, not to mention my allergies have been terrible! After these walks, I sleep soundly, which is a welcome relief. Today it was so warm that the chocolates Thomas brought melted outside! I had to eat them quickly before they were ruined."

Emma looked up, feeling baffled by what she'd just read. Jack opened his mouth to say something, then closed it as Ezekial spoke up. "I think the chocolates are drugged. I also think these so-called walks were a way for Thomas to get out on the grounds to search for a hiding spot for the gold, while walking with his own built-in tour guide."

Emma sat back against the couch and nodded slowly. "Do you know anything about the grounds of the house?"

Ezekial rubbed his chin and stared out the window, deep in thought. "The house was in the family for generations. They founded the town, so there isn't much to the property, other than the house itself. The family has had money going back as far as anyone can remember. So, they built the house, but there wasn't a barn or stable.

Probably an outhouse on the property, but what you see is pretty much what you get."

"I don't even remember seeing an outhouse, or anything resembling one," Jack said.

"I just wonder if she ever suspected that Thomas had ill intentions," Emma said. "She seemed so lonely and so desperate for company that I wonder if she overlooked any danger Thomas might have posed."

"Let's keep reading," Jack suggested.

"May fifteenth," Emma began. "I fear that I am becoming ill. I've been sleeping more and more, and today when I got up, I almost blacked out. I had to sit down quickly and was shaking and sweaty. Maybe my nerves are just bothered because of having constant dreams that my gold coins are being stolen. It's silly because no one else even knows about these coins. I keep them because Dakota gave them to me, and they were sentimental to him. I've moved all the coins to the compartment behind the fake books in the library and had just put the last one in place yesterday when Thomas came into the room. I haven't told him about the gold and am not really sure why. It's my last connection to Dakota, and feels almost like a secret that only he and I share."

Emma paused here. "Oh goodness, how sad. She's in this huge house all alone, possibly hallucinating or being poisoned, or both, and she still misses her dead fiance."

She flipped the page and continued reading.

"May eighteenth. Perhaps I jinxed myself in the last diary entry. I was in the library today, looking at the coins. I also put some jewelry that Dakota had given me in the same box. It's probably not worth much money, as it was just some Indian turquoise jewelry that belonged to his mother. Sometimes I feel so strongly that Dakota's spirit is here in the house with me. I was feeling especially nostalgic today, probably because I was looking at the jewelry. I was just putting everything back in the box, tucking the chain and the charm and the coins into place, when I heard Thomas on the stairs. I hurriedly put the box in its hiding spot, but I was covering it with the fake books when he walked in the door. He startled me so much I must have jumped a foot in the air. He said he was at the front door for a few minutes, and since I didn't answer, he came in to make sure I was okay. I didn't hear him on the stairs, and by the time I realized he was here, it was too late. I just wanted the hiding spot to be a secret, and now I feel like it's not as special as it once was."

Emma stopped reading again and looked at Jack and Ezekial.

"Good grief!" Ezekial exclaimed. "He wasn't trying very hard at the front door. The family had a doorbell put in. It seems he intended to sneak up on her."

Emma raised her eyebrows. "Do you think he knew about the gold?"

"Or at least suspected it?" Jack asked.

"I absolutely do," Ezekial said. He crossed the room again and went to the desk where he had retrieved the book earlier. He rummaged around in a drawer, then pulled out a rolled-up document of some sort. "These are the original house plans for Isabel's mansion. They show the hiding spot in the library, as well as some windows that were closed in."

He brought the rolled-up document over and untied the string that was holding it in place. Then he and Jack unrolled the paper and held opposite sides so they could all look at the document in full.

"I think we should go to the house again." Jack said. "Ezekial, would you like to come with us?"

Ezekial had already started rolling up the paper. "I'd love to," he said, heading for the door.

The three of them walked through town on a path that was becoming all too familiar to Emma: through the town, across the footbridge, and up the hill to the big mansion. Ezekial pushed the doorbell on the side of the front door, and the chimes echoed through the large house. He looked over his shoulder and gave Jack and Emma a smirk. The chimes were still reverberating when they entered the front door and headed to the library on the third floor. Ezekial pulled out his floorplan and after a few seconds of consulting, he directed Jack and Emma to the spot on the shelf where the fake books were. Jack pulled the books out and placed them on the desk behind him. There was a small metal closure in the wall at the height of the bookshelf. Jack grasped the handle and pulled open a compartment. The hinges squeaked in protest. The compartment was empty.

Chapter 8: Confronting the Corrupt Businessman

Jack, Ezekial, and Emma all looked at each other. The silence in the room was deafening.

"Does this mean Thomas took the money?" Emma asked in a whisper, her blue eyes wide.

"Or he at the very least knows where it is," Ezekial said. "I think we need to talk to Sheriff Campbell. This seems like it could be evidence, or at least a clue that would lead us to something significant."

Emma nodded solemnly. Jack wordlessly closed the metal door and replaced the fake books. The three of them descended the stairs and made their way back down the hill, across the footbridge, and through the dusty streets. The sheriff's office was located on the opposite end of town, nestled between an old bakery and a shoe store. Looking through the window, they could see Sheriff Campbell sitting at his desk, typing frantically. Jack rapped on the door and pushed it open, causing the bell above to tinkle merrily.

"Hello!" Sheriff Campbell called out, banging out a few more keys on the typewriter and then standing to greet them.

"Hello," Emma responded, walking towards his desk. Jack and Ezekial followed her.

"Well, what brings you all here today? Looks serious. Please, have a seat." Sheriff Campbell gestured toward the chairs that lined the half wall opposite his desk.

The trio sat down and looked at the sheriff, who was watching them expectantly. He was tapping a pencil on the edge of the desk to a rhythm only he could hear.

"We think we might have some clues to Isabel's whereabouts," Jack said. He gestured to the diary that Emma was holding.

Sheriff Campbell stopped drumming his pencil and held it mid-air. "How?" he asked. "What has developed since the last time I talked to you all?"

Emma showed the sheriff the diary while Jack started to explain about their trek to the house and the missing gold coins that had been hidden in the library. Sheriff Campbell narrowed his eyes and chewed on the tip of his pencil for several seconds after the story was finished. Suddenly, his eyes widened and he jumped up, cowboy boots clomping across the wooden floor. He pushed the door open to a back room, and the sounds of a file cabinet drawer opening and then slamming shut again could be heard in the main visitor's area. He reappeared carrying a manila folder that was bulging with papers and dropped it on his desk, causing a little puff of dust to blow up.

"This," he said. "Is Thomas Benson's file for all the permits and businesses he has invested in. I seem to remember him coming in at the beginning of June, paying for a deed to one of the vacant buildings a little farther out of town, the barn and sheds that Earl used long ago when he had the blacksmith business."

Sheriff Campbell opened the file and pulled out a receipt. He examined it, then passed it across the desk to Emma. Jack and Ezekial leaned closer to look. The receipt was dated June tenth. Emma raised her eyebrows.

"He came in, claiming he had 'just come into some money,'" the sheriff continued. "I didn't pay him a lot of attention. He has business deals all over. He paid for the permit and the sales tax and then left. Now I wonder if this money he came into was actually the gold coins he took from Isabel."

He ruffled through some more papers in the folder. "Here's another one," he said. "This is dated two years prior, in December. This is the tax receipt for the pharmacy, which he never actually opened."

"Wait a minute," Ezekial interrupted. "There are tax receipts for several businesses and buildings here, but none of these places are open.

He bought a bunch of buildings, or paid the back taxes on them, but for what?"

Sheriff Campbell ruffled through some more papers and found copies of other deeds and tax receipts: one for the tack shop, one for a butcher shop, and one for a bakery. None of these businesses were open or even close to being operable.

"Some of these dates back years. Quite a few of these are from before I became sheriff. It might be interesting to see the dates on some of them." Sheriff Campbell looked at Ezekial. "Do you remember when Dakota died? I remember it being right before Christmas, perhaps two years ago?"

Ezekial pursed his lips. "Yes, right before Christmas. Two years before Isabel disappeared."

The sheriff looked at the paperwork for the pharmacy again. He held it out for Emma, Jack, and Ezekial to see. "Yes. This is for the week right after Dakota died. I remember it because we had the ice storm that year and had to wait on the burial."

Ezekial was talking fast now with excitement over the new information. "Is it possible that the pharmacy acquisition has anything to do with Dakota's death? The timing is quite a coincidence, especially since Isabel disappeared right before he made another purchase. I know he owns several businesses in this town, but they clearly don't generate enough revenue to purchase more businesses. What are the odds that he just happened to come into more money shortly after the two people who had money died or disappeared?"

The sheriff nodded. "I think you're on to something. I can get a warrant issued and go talk to the bank, and they can show me the business accounts." He stood abruptly, putting on his coat and grabbing his hat, plunking it on his head and pushing his chair behind the desk. "This might take me all afternoon. Let's meet tomorrow at the inn for breakfast, shall we?"

Ezekial, Jack, and Emma shuffled to the door and stood on the sidewalk, wishing Sheriff Campbell safe travels. Emma wasn't sure how she was going to survive the suspense for the rest of the day.

***

Emma once again tossed and turned all night, feeling sure that they were all closer to finding the mysterious lost treasure and the missing Isabel. She woke early, dressed quickly, and darted down the stairs. To her surprise, the dining room was already full. Sheriff Campbell, Jack, and Ezekial sat at one table. Sarah bustled about, pouring coffee and juice for everyone, and Nancy was helping bring out plates heaped with food. Emma took a seat at the table next to Jack and reached for a blueberry muffin.

When Sarah and Nancy sat down at the table, Sheriff Campbell spoke up. "Okay," he said. "We're all here. I got the warrant yesterday and went straight to the bank. I was able to speak to the manager, who was very accommodating and showed me the ledger for Thomas Benson's business account." He wrung his hands together and looked around the table at everyone, taking a deep breath. "Thomas made two substantial deposits, both in gold coins. The dates coincide with both the disappearance of Isabel and the death of Dakota."

He looked sullen as he sat down, allowing everyone to take in the information they had just heard. A silence settled over the table.

Jack spoke up. "So, now what? We have the proof we need. What do we do next?"

Everyone looked around the table at each other. No one spoke.

"We have to do something," Jack said. "If for no other reason than we might be able to find Isabel. We know that Thomas plans to take over the saloon if he can get the back taxes together. Who knows what he might do next to come up with some money? For all we know, any one of us could be in danger."

"I think we should just confront him," Nancy said softly.

"What can he do if we all show up together?" Sarah asked.

Emma looked at her. Sarah was serious but hadn't been in the saloon when Thomas and his men had shown up, and that was terrifying.

Nancy let out a giggle. She picked the muffin up off her plate and dropped it with a thud. "We could use these as weapons."

Everyone at the table laughed nervously.

"For real," Nancy said, the most unlikely soldier of all. "I think we should all go to Benson Enterprises. There are six of us, and there are only three of them. Let's do it."

"Just like that?" Emma asked. "It's that simple?"

Everyone at the table looked at each other. Jack shrugged, then stood up. "Let's go!"

The mismatched group stood up, walked out of the dining room, and down the sidewalk to Benson Enterprises. Jack and Emma led the way, followed by Sheriff Campbell, Ezekial, Sarah, and Nancy, whom Emma noticed really was carrying the muffins in a basket. When Jack and Emma got to the front door, they stepped aside and let Sheriff Campbell pass through. Emma wasn't sure what she expected Benson Enterprises to look like, but what she saw was not it. Two desks sat in the front room, one for each of Thomas's men, she assumed. The walls were an indistinct grayish color, and each of the desks had their own filing cabinet, cup of pencils, legal pad, and calendar.

Sheriff Campbell led them all down the hall, then made a sharp right. He did not stop when he got to the office at the end of the hallway, but instead barged right through the door and stood in front of Thomas's desk.

"Can I help you?" Thomas asked, leaning back in his chair. Ever the suave businessman, he was not deterred as he gazed at the mismatched group of people.

"I think that you can," Jack said. "We have reason to believe that you know of Isabel's whereabouts. We also have reason to believe that you know how Dakota died, and that you stole the gold coins from them in order to fund some of your operations."

Thomas's face reddened slightly, but he remained unmoved. "You can prove no such things."

"We have Isabel's diary," Emma spoke up. "And between the diary and the evidence we have pieced together, you look extremely guilty."

Thomas stood up. "I'm sure you're mistaken. Let's go into the larger room where we can all talk."

Emma bristled at his syrupy sweet voice. Either he had something planned for them, or he knew he was caught and was trying to weasel his way out. Or both.

Thomas shut his office door and led the group down the hall to the big room they had first walked into. As soon as they were all inside, he reached into his pocket and pulled out a whistle. He blew one sharp breath into it, and a shrill blast emerged. His two henchmen came running out of another room. Sheriff Campbell darted to the front door to prevent Thomas from escaping.

"It's no use, Thomas," he said. "Tell us what you've done with Isabel. The bank has proof that you deposited the gold coins into your account."

"We think you know where Isabel is," Jack added.

They all stared at Thomas for what seemed like an eternity. "You don't know anything!" he growled.

"But we do," Sheriff Campbell said. "We've been reading Isabel's diary. Were you actually sneaking around her property at night? Furthermore, were you just barging in her house unannounced? That's trespassing."

"You can't prove that," sneered Thomas.

"But we can," Emma said, waving the diary in the air. "We've been reading this diary since I found it."

His face turned pale. "Where did you find that?"

Emma was about to speak up when Sheriff Campbell held his hand up, the universal sign for her to stop.

"Where do you think we found it?" the sheriff asked.

"I...I don't know," Thomas stammered.

"How do you feel knowing that you stole money from a woman who has already lost so much?" Sheriff Campbell demanded.

Thomas looked around at Sheriff Campbell, who was still blocking the door, Emma, Jack, Ezekial, Sarah, and Nancy. Sarah had an expression of motherly concern on her face. Nancy had the basket of muffins slung over one arm, poised and ready to begin throwing them. Suddenly, he motioned to his two buddies and abruptly turned, most likely heading for the back door. His men started to follow him, but all were quickly distracted when Nancy started launching muffins at their heads. Jack stood in the doorway leading to the back of the building and crossed his arms. Sheriff Campbell quickly crossed the room and stood next to Jack.

"We know exactly what you've done," Sheriff Campbell said. "It's time to just admit to everything."

"You can't prove it!" Thomas shouted. "This is all just conspiracy! You have no right to arrest me because I deposited gold into my bank account. You don't know where that gold came from!" He stared at the group gathered before him and growled, "Get. Out."

In one swift move, there was a crash and a clatter as Thomas and his henchmen darted through the crowd and burst out the door, running down the street.

Chapter 9: Treasure Hunt

Sheriff Campbell raced out the door in hot pursuit of the men, while everyone else looked behind him, dumbfounded. Nancy and Sarah seemed shaken up, and both women said they were heading home to regroup. Ezekial went to document the day's events in case they were ever needed in court, which left Jack and Emma standing on the sidewalk in front of Benson Enterprises.

"Do you think the hidden treasure is real?" Emma asked, glancing around nervously.

Jack exhaled. "I don't know," he said. But there's only one way to find out. Let's see if we can find something, or at least a clue."

"How do we even know where to start?" Emma asked.

"Ezekial believes it's legitimate, which makes me think there's evidence somewhere. The tribe that Dakota was associated with is a few miles from here. We could ride the horses there, but then we would have to hike over some treacherous rocks. Are you up for the challenge?"

Emma nodded. "Let's go."

They made their way to the stable and saddled their horses, then started the journey out of town. It felt quite different than when Emma had first arrived with Cinnamon, as the terrain was rocky and she had to slow her horse down several times to redirect her or to help her gain footing. Cinnamon's gait was becoming less and less gleeful the farther they went. Finally, Jack whistled to her and signaled for them to stop. Emma pulled Cinnamon's reins and slowed her to barely a walk, giving soothing words of encouragement.

"I think this is as far as the horses can go," he said. "We'll have to tie them here."

Emma looked around. They were standing on a steep hill, with huge rucks jutting from the ground. She looked in the direction from which they had come and couldn't believe they had traveled so far. The abandoned houses and stores looked like small dots from this distance.

"According to legend, the natives hid in these hills for as long as possible, trying to protect the tribe from the white men who were invading their territory," Jack began. "This is the tribe that Dakota is from."

"Wow," Emma said, looking around. "I can't imagine staying here and sleeping on this rocky ground."

Jack agreed. "Legend has it that the tribe made hammocks to suspend from the trees. They felt that the hammock brought them back to their roots, as the swaying mimicked being cocooned in the womb." he shrugged. "It makes sense, if you think about it."

Emma nodded and looked around again. They had reached the top of the hill and were met with a line of trees. From where she sat on Cinnamon's back, she could look down the hill and see the town. She feared if she went much farther, the line of trees would turn into a forest, and the idea of venturing into the forest with no weapons suddenly seemed terrifying to her.

"Come on," Jack said, looking up towards the sky. "We better take advantage of all the sunlight we can get."

Emma gave Cinnamon a small kiss on the snout for good luck, then reassured her that they would be back soon.

She followed Jack into the woods. As they walked, the light that filtered through the trees seemed to grow more and more dim, and the temperature dropped a few degrees. Jack noticed that Emma was shivering. "Cold?" he asked, narrowing his eyes in a concerned expression.

"No," Emma said. She took a few more steps. "Just thinking about what could be in these woods waiting for us."

Jack smiled. "During the day, probably not too much. The Indian tribe who lived here has moved on. The land and resources became scarce. A few of the descendants live in town. We will be out of here well before dark."

Emma nodded, reassured but still not totally convinced.

"What are we looking for?" She asked. "How do we know where the treasure is supposed to be?"

"We should come to a small clearing eventually. It's a spot in the woods where there are no rocks. Most likely, the rocks were cleared for this very reason- to bury the treasure, if it exists. When we get to the edge of the rocks, the treasure should be twenty paces inside the clear area."

"Hmm," Emma said. "That's a lot of uncertainty."

"Yes," Jack agreed. "But wouldn't it be amazing to be a part of history if we find it?"

She couldn't disagree. They trudged on in silence, Emma dodging rocks and Jack extending his arm every so often when the terrain got too unsteady. They had been walking for quite some time when out of nowhere, Emma reached out and gripped Jack's arm, her fingers turning white from the force.

"Look," she whispered, gesturing wildly.

Directly in front of them was a manmade firepit. The stones were arranged in two layers in a perfect circle. A single trail of smoke drifted up into the sky, thin and wispy. No one was around now, but someone had been there recently.

"Where do you think they could be?" Emma asked.

Jack looked around, his blue eyes wide. "More importantly, who else is out here?"

Emma shook her head and pulled the diary out of the leather knapsack she was carrying. She flipped through the pages, desperate for a clue as to who else might have known about the treasure or about Dakota's family. Wedged in a back page, folded in half, was a piece of paper.

"What's this?" she asked, holding it out to Jack.

He took the paper from her, holding it gingerly between his thumb and forefinger. Together they peered closely at what seemed to be a drawing of some sort, although a corner of the paper had been ripped off and the ink was faded in some parts. Jack turned the paper clockwise, then counterclockwise several times.

"What are we looking at?" he muttered.

"I think it's a map," Emma suggested. "But what are these shapes?"

The map appeared to have symbols drawn in no rhyme or reason. There were five oblong shapes, each with a circle at various points inside.

Jack drew in a sharp breath. "They're feathers," he said, dumbfounded. These are peacock feathers. There are wild peacocks at the Monroe mansion. The gold must be hidden there somewhere."

Emma's jaw dropped.

"Let's go!" Jack stage-whispered, ushering Emma back the way they came.

The pair journeyed back down the hill, each step seeming to take longer than the last. Finally reaching the horses, they galloped away as fast as possible.

When they got back into town, they slowed the horses to a trot.

"What does this mean?" Emma asked.

"I'm not sure," Jack said. "But the gold was definitely at the Monroe Mansion at some point in time. I'm sure of it."

Chapter 10: Haunted by Secrets

Emma stood looking out the window of the saloon, onto the deserted street. Sheriff Campbell had caught Thomas and placed him in the jail cell behind the sheriff's office, but she couldn't calm her nerves enough to relax and enjoy dinner. She kept sitting down, then jumping up and darting to the window, sure that she heard something in the street. Thomas's henchmen had disappeared, running down the street in completely different directions. No one had seen or heard from them since, and even though several days had passed, Emma was firmly convinced that they would show up at the saloon out of nowhere, trying to finish his mission, whatever that seemed to be.

Jack sighed. "I thought that Thomas's buddies would somehow make an appearance. Even if they didn't come to the saloon, maybe they would've been slinking back through town. At this point, since we haven't seen them in a few days, I really doubt they'll just show up out of nowhere," Jack said, trying to be reassuring.

"You're probably right," Emma said, turning from the window and letting the gingham curtains fall. "This is bringing me back to my childhood."

She sat down at the table again with Jack. He laid down his fork and raised his eyebrows, waiting for her to continue. Emma in turn picked up her fork and started pushing her food around her plate.

"Do you want to tell me about it?" he asked.

She sighed. "I had a friend who disappeared when we were just young girls. It was very much like Isabel's disappearance. When I first found the diary, I started having dreams and flashbacks about her. Jenny and I were much younger though, just grade school kids. She was never found, and I've always blamed myself. I stayed home from school the day she disappeared because I had a fever. Jenny disappeared sometime on her walk home alone."

Jack pushed his plate toward the center of the table and leaned forward on his elbows. "Wow," he said. "I had no idea."

Emma looked down at her hands folded in her lap. "Yeah. I don't talk about it too often, and try my best to not think about it, but sometimes it resurfaces and hits me hard. The last couple of nights I've been so exhausted that I didn't even have any dreams. But it definitely came back today. Thomas knows where Isabel is. I just feel it. The same way that someone in our small town knew where Jenny was."

"I'm sure you're right," Jack said, placing his hand over Emma's.

Emma squeezed his hand with hers. "Yes. I think a big reason as to why I went into investigative journalism was to help other families who had big mysteries to solve. Kind of as a way to fix what I couldn't fix in my own life, I guess."

Jack nodded. "That makes sense. I wonder if now, as an adult with your investigative skills, could you go back and try to solve that mystery?"

Emma nodded slowly. "I never really thought about that. As a kid, I felt so guilty. And it seemed so final. She was just gone. We were school age children, still playing with dolls and buying penny candy from the store when she disappeared. I've always been stuck in that feeling guilty rut. We used to go to this lake on the way home from school and feed the ducks our leftover lunch scraps. Bread crusts and things like that. I was the one who always wanted to go. I used to beg Jenny to go to the lake on the days it was too cold or raining, so sure if we didn't go that the ducks would go to bed hungry that night. After she disappeared, I would walk to the lake by myself and just stare at my reflection. There was once two of us reflected in the water, and then it was only me. I think I felt her loss the most those days."

Jack was quiet as he listened. "I'm so sorry," he said softly.

Emma realized that these past few days with the diary, Thomas and his men, searching the Monroe mansion for clues, and all the detective work she and the others had done were really dredging up some memories.

"I used to stare into the water and talk to her, as if she were still right there at the lake with me. I did this for years. Much longer than I should have. One time, shortly after she had disappeared, I walked to the lake, and as soon as I got to the edge and was staring at my reflection, I thought to myself 'Jenny's here.' It's like the thought just washed over me. I was so sad for the rest of the day. I started going back to the lake, just so I could talk to her."

Emma could clearly tell Jack was thinking about something. She hoped she hadn't overshared. She had told this story to her mother, who said she must never bring that up again because if anyone knew she was talking to herself at the lake she would seem either crazy or guilty. As a child, Emma hadn't understood that either.

After a few seconds of awkward silence, Emma spoke up. "I'm sorry," she said. "That was a lot."

Jack cleared his throat and shook his head. "No, it's okay, really."

The two pushed their food around on their plates not really eating, until Jack broke the silence. "I lost my parents at a young age. It was a housefire. My sister and I had gone to stay with our grandparents, just a few streets over. Authorities think they had left an oil lamp on overnight and that the cat knocked it over."

Now it was Emma's turn to be surprised. "Oh no," she breathed. "That's horrible."

"Yeah," Jack continued. "They died in their sleep. At least that's what the authorities said. We were both really little, like first and second grade. We ended up going back to live with our grandparents. But the fact that I was so close when it happened and couldn't do anything about it has always haunted me."

"Oh Jack," Emma gushed. "I'm so sorry."

He gave a sad smile. "It really brought my sister and I together, that's for sure. I wonder what would have happened had we been home at the time. Would we have woken up? The cat's name was Patches, and he always slept with me at night. If I had been home, he probably would have slept in my bed and the fire never would have started."

Jack wiped the corner of his eyes and gave a little laugh. "I'm sorry," he said. "I haven't talked about this in a long time."

"It's okay," Emma said softly. "But you can't blame yourself. What if the cat had seen a squirrel outside or a mouse running around the house at night? What if there was a shadow outside and he got spooked? It could just as easily have happened another time when you all were home."

Jack shuddered. "Yes. But you know we don't think like that when we're in the situation. It's so easy to take the blame and feel like we're the ones who could've saved the day."

"I know that all too well," Emma agreed.

He took her hand and pulled her to a standing position, putting his other arm around her waist, and pulled her close. The two stood like that for a few seconds, staring into each other's eyes, until Jack tilted his head down to kiss Emma lightly. When her lips met his, she felt electricity running through her veins. As he continued to kiss her, Emma hoped that the part for her stagecoach would get delayed just a little bit longer.

Chapter 11: Unraveling the Ghost Town's Secrets

The next morning, Emma found herself awake before the sun was fully up. She had barely slept last night, but instead tossed and turned, replaying Jack's sweet kiss over and over again in her mind. When he walked her back to the inn, he had kissed her again, on the front porch under the full moon. They had promised to meet at breakfast in the morning so that they could go through the diary in more detail and try to piece some things together.

Emma flounced down the stairs and into the dining room, where Sarah was already waiting.

"Well, you seem to be in a good mood this morning," Sarah said, winking.

Emma blushed and sat down at the table. Soon they were joined by Jack, the sheriff, Nancy, and Ezekial. The crew began to discuss Thomas's henchmen, and Sheriff Campbell confirmed that no one had reported seeing them yet.

Suddenly, an idea came to Emma.

"I remember you guys saying at one point that Dakota, Isabel's fiancé, died by falling into an abandoned mine. Do you think there's any way that Thomas's men could be hiding there? A lot of these mines have shafts and caves that lead to all kinds of places."

Sheriff Campbell nodded his head slowly and took a long drink of coffee. "Anything is possible. I checked the perimeter of the mine when I was looking for Thomas, but there were no recent footprints and no traces of anyone. That doesn't mean that someone couldn't have gone in after I was there."

Emma looked around the table. "It's worth a thought I guess."

"Yes, I agree," Sheriff Campbell said. "Unfortunately, Thomas won't give up any information about their whereabouts, and I have to process some court papers today in order to get him prosecuted." He pulled a little pad of paper and a pencil from his front pocket and scratched a note hastily. "I'll definitely check that out."

When everyone was finished eating, Sheriff Campbell, Ezekial, Nancy, and Sarah got up to go their separate ways, all heading out to complete their respective tasks for the day, which left only Emma and Jack at the table. Emma suddenly found herself getting nervous and felt the contents of her stomach churning. Jack looked across the table and smiled, his eyes sparkling.

"What do you say you and I go to the cave and check it out?" he asked, giving her a wink. "It's a beautiful day, and there's no harm in taking a ride to explore."

Emma smiled. "I'd love to. And I know Cinnamon would enjoy an adventure."

He stood up from the table and offered her his hand. Together, they made their way to the stable and saddled up both Cinnamon and Jack's horse Daisy. Emma made sure to tuck the diary in her saddle bag, just in case there were some clues they hadn't gotten to yet. They were so close to finding something that would be helpful. She could feel it.

The horses started off on an easy gallop, both of them tossing their heads and shaking their manes with delight as they trotted into the bright sun and up the steep hill that would lead to the abandoned mine. They crested the hill and slowed the horses down, gazing out into the vast distance.

"Wow," Emma said. "This is beautiful."

"It sure is," Jack agreed. "Kind of bittersweet. The scenery and the town itself are gorgeous, but there are some things here that people would love to forget."

"Should we take a look around to see what we can find?" Emma asked.

He nodded and dismounted, then brought both horses to a grove of trees and tied their leads. They walked down the dusty trail that led directly into the mine.

"Sheriff Campbell was right," Emma noted. "It does seem as if no one has been here in a while."

"Yes," Jack agreed. "I wonder what we'll find when we get closer to the bottom though?"

Emma looked around her and then down to the bottom of the trail. There was nothing but dust, tumbleweeds, and scraggly patches of grass for as far as she could see. Every once in a while, a gust of wind would come and ruffle her skirt or blow whisps of hair over her shoulders.

"This place is creepy. Exactly why it would make a good hiding spot. How far do you think we should go before we give up?" she asked.

Jack looked around. "I'm not sure. The trail ends a little farther down, right at the edge of the mine. Let's see what we can find."

The pair continued walking, with the trail getting steeper and steeper the closer they got to the mine. Emma stopped short and reached out to grab Jack's arm.

"What was that?" she whispered, pointing to something shiny hidden in a tuft of grass.

He pried himself loose from her grip and bent to inspect what she was pointing at. "It hasn't been here too long, or it would be dusty," he observed, parting the long blades of grass and pulling an empty tin can out, along with a fork and spoon.

"Hmmm." Emma looked around, suddenly afraid that someone could jump out of nowhere to confront them. "That looks like the food of someone who's in hiding."

Jack also looked around, then placed the utensils in the empty can, face down, and held the can gingerly between his thumb and forefinger. "This might be the closest thing we have to evidence. I'll hang onto it."

After scouring the area for any more items and finding nothing, they continued down the path. They walked for quite some time, stopping every so often to take a closer look at their surroundings. They had reached the edge of the trail overlooking the mine when Emma noticed something.

"Look!" She whispered excitedly. "Is that an opening in the rocks?"

Jack looked to where she was pointing. He squinted his eyes, but it was hard to tell if it was an opening or just an abnormal shape in the walls of the mine. He grabbed Emma's hand and the two made their way around the edge of the mine, carefully stepping over loose rocks and uneven ground. The climb was treacherous, but once they reached the spot where Emma had pointed, they could see it was indeed an opening.

"What should we do?" Emma asked, looking up at the sun. It was well past noon, and even though they still had a lot of daylight left, she was worried about leaving the horses tied by themselves. She said as much to Jack.

He looked at the sky, then up the trail where they had just come from, then to the opening in the wall. "Let's just try to look inside," he said. "If we find anything of substance, we'll take what we can back to Sheriff Campbell."

"Okay," Emma agreed.

The opening was small, with barely room for one person at a time to squeeze in sideways.

"I'll go first," Jack said, setting the empty tin can on the ground.

He turned sideways and shimmied through, and Emma followed, her stomach churning and her palms sweaty. Once they had squeezed through the narrow entrance, they found themselves in a small cave. Emma blinked, waiting for her eyes to adjust to the dim light. The sun was angled just enough to cast a dim glow inside, and once her vision adjusted, it was obvious that someone had been there recently. An Indian blanked was folded on the floor, and more tin cans were lined up against the wall.

Jack walked over to where the blanket was and inspected the rows of cans stacked neatly. He felt along the wall of the cave, and his hand slipped into another opening.

"There's a tunnel!" He whispered to Emma. "This leads somewhere."

"Don't go through it!" Emma whispered nervously. "We can bring back a lantern and maybe Sheriff Campbell."

Jack hesitated, but it was hard for Emma to see his face in the dim light. She couldn't tell if he had found something else or if he was contemplating going through the tunnel to the other side.

Jack reached around, waving his hands frantically, then stopped suddenly.

"What?" Emma hissed.

"I found something else in here. It's soft, like a blanket. I think." Jack gave a tug and freed whatever he was trying to grab. From the way his arm jerked, Emma assumed the blanket was stuck or attached to something.

He pulled the blanket out and then stepped into the dim lighting. He gasped.

"Emma. We need to go," he said, taking two paces back and grabbing her hand to pull her forward. "It's not a blanket. It's Isabel's shawl. She wore this all the time. It came from Dakota's family."

Emma reached out to touch the shawl, then dropped it quickly.

"What if she's in there?" Emma shuddered at the thought. "We have to find out. I've always blamed myself for Jenny's disappearance. We can't leave if there's a chance we could save Isabel."

Jack stopped in his tracks. "Okay, how about this," he began slowly. I'll go into the tunnel and feel around for anything else I can find. If I can't find any substantial evidence, we go straight to Sheriff Campbell. Deal?"

Emma nodded, then realized Jack couldn't see her in the dark. "Okay, deal," she said hesitantly.

Jack felt his way back to the tunnel and disappeared from Emma's sight. "Jack?" she called. "Are you okay?"

"Yes," he called back. His voice echoed in the cave.

"Keep talking to me so I know you're okay," Emma said.

"Okay," Jack answered. "Feeling around. Still nothing in here." He paused after every few words, waiting for the echo to catch up.

Emma heard a noise, and then Jack called out "I think I found something!"

All she could hear was scuffling, like the sound of objects being scooted across the floor.

"It's a box of some sort," Jack called. "I'm trying to scoot it out of the tunnel."

Emma waited for what seemed like an eternity for him to push whatever he had found into the space where she was standing. Finally Jack emerged, pushing a box across the floor. It wasn't a box after all, but more of a trunk, the wooden kind that had metal hinges and a closure that snapped in front. In the shadows it looked beat up, like it had been loaded and unloaded a few too many times from the back of a moving stagecoach.

Jack gave the box one final shove and then stood up, panting. "I have no idea what this could be. Something like this doesn't just appear in the cave. The question is, how did it get here?"

"Is there an opening on the other side?" Emma asked.

"There has to be," Jack said. "I bet Ezekial would know the lay of the land better than I would."

He unhooked the latches and slowly lifted the lid, peering in carefully. He gasped, then slammed the lid shut again.

"It's gold!" Jack exclaimed. "There's a pile of coins in this trunk."

Emma rushed over to the trunk and he opened the lid for her to look inside.

Emma shrieked, then reached up to slam the lid shut again. "This is the gold that Isabel was writing about! It has to be!"

"This gold must have belonged to Dakota's family. I don't know why it's in this cave," Jack said as he lifted the lid for the third time and looked at all the gold coins. He bent over and used his hand to sweep through the large pile. "Well look at that," he said, holding up a few pieces of paper. "There were some papers mixed in with the gold."

Emma took the papers and held them up to the light, but she could not make out any words other than "Shipment Delayed" on one document and "Eviction Notice" on another.

"There has to be more to this. These documents were hidden for a reason," Jack said. I vote we put the chest back but take whatever documents we can find. They've been buried here for a while. I doubt anyone will come back for them overnight."

Emma didn't like the idea of taking the documents, in case whoever hid them came back looking for them. The only other option was to leave them and return with Sheriff Campbell, but if whoever left these items came back, there was always the risk that the chest would be moved to a location that she and Jack wouldn't be able to find. And she definitely didn't like that idea, not with the shawl and the documents having been hidden in the same room. So she agreed, and Jack pushed the chest back to its spot in the tunnel.

They began the hike back up the trail to the horses, documents and tin can in hand. Emma was silent on the walk, exhausted from the adrenaline rush of finding the cave, the chest, and Isabel's shawl. The horses stamped their feet impatiently when they saw Emma and Jack walking back toward them. They rode the horses straight to the sheriff's office, where they found Sheriff Campbell sitting at his desk, filling out paperwork. He looked up when he saw them walking in the door.

"What can I do for you guys? It looks like you found something," he said.

"We definitely did," Jack said. "We haven't gotten to look at these documents extensively, but we found Isabel's shawl and a tin can and utensils, so we think someone has been near the mine after all."

Sheriff Campbell motioned to the chairs in front of his desk, and Emma and Jack sat down to tell him about finding the tin can, the hidden cave, and the chest of gold. Jack took the documents from his pocket and flattened them out on the desk.

Sheriff Campbell frowned and picked up the document that said, "Eviction Notice." He glanced through it briefly, then set it back down again.

"This is fraud," he said indignantly. "This is the so-called eviction notice for the general store. It was never filed here, which makes sense now, because when the Hudson's left town, they did so rather suddenly. When I asked where they were going, they gave a vague answer, probably thinking I'd had evicted them."

The three pored over the other documents, and Sheriff Campbell found legal fault with almost every one of them. There were more false eviction notices, and delayed shipment notices for the stores, which caused owners to lose money and be late on their rent payments, most of which were paid to Benson Enterprises.

"Well, I'll be," the sheriff whispered, staring at the papers. "Everyone left this town because they were being forced out by Thomas."

Chapter 12: Betrayal and Redemption

Emma retired early that evening, hoping to get some much-needed sleep. She dozed off instantly, but after a few hours, was wide awake with her mind reeling. The day was replaying itself in one big loop. The hike up the hill with the horses, the exploration of the cave, the ride back, and the time in Sheriff Campbell's Office were all fresh in her mind. She was sure they had missed something, but a part of her also wondered if she was only feeling that way because she wanted to solve Isabel's disappearance and redeem herself for not being able to solve Jenny's disappearance. How did she always get involved in these situations, anyway?

After more tossing and turning, Emma finally got up. With all the events of the past few days, there hadn't been a lot of time to read the rest of the diary. There had to be something they were missing. She got out of bed and stumbled her way across the room to turn on the lamp, rubbing her eyes and pulling her robe around her, then sat down to read. The next few entries were about the same as before: Thomas had come to visit, he brought her gifts each time, they went on carriage rides and walks around the extensive property that surrounded the Monroe mansion. Emma was just about to close the diary when she got to one entry that seemed unusual. It was dated July 3. She skimmed through the entry quickly, thinking she had misread it. Sure enough: On July third, Charlotte Rose had paid Isabel a visit unexpectedly. From what she could gather in the diary entry, the two had been friendly since Dakota was Charlotte Rose's brother. Although the visit was unexpected, Isabel had been happy to see her. In fact, one of the lines was "I don't know why it has taken Charlotte so long to visit." What seemed to be disturbing to Emma was that Thomas showed up while Charlotte was there.

Although Emma did not necessarily like Charlotte because of her flirtations with Jack, she didn't exactly think Charlotte was evil. Was there some sort of connection here, or was it just an odd coincidence? Charlotte was scheduled to leave town in the next day or two, and while Emma had thought it was odd that Charlotte hadn't been around much lately, she had been happy to have Jack to herself again, so she didn't question it. Emma read and reread the diary entry, desperate to find a clue that she had missed. Finding nothing, she got dressed and ready to go down to breakfast. Maybe there was a chance they could catch Charlotte before she left town, but what would they say? Just because Thomas happened to show up at the same time that Charlotte was there didn't necessarily mean anything. Charlotte and Isabel would have been sisters-in-law, had Dakota not died. The visit wasn't that out of the ordinary. Still, she couldn't shake the feeling that something was off.

Emma laid back down for what she intended to be just a few moments but fell asleep until well after breakfast was over. She made the short walk over to the saloon, where Jack and Nancy were setting up for the day.

"Morning, sunshine!" Nancy called cheerfully across the saloon when Emma entered.

"It's about time!" Jack echoed, laughing good-naturedly.

"I can't believe I slept this long!" Emma exclaimed. "I woke up in the middle of the night and started reading more of the diary, then just dozed off again."

She sat down at the bar and accepted the cup of coffee Nancy gave her. Emma was debating how to bring up the fact that she believed Charlotte Rose possibly had a connection to Thomas. If she said something, would everyone just think she was jealous of Charlotte and trying to paint her in a bad light? But if she didn't say anything, and this was a missing piece of the puzzle, would she regret not speaking up?

"All right, spill it," Nancy said. "What's eating you?"

Emma took a deep breath, then pulled out the diary. "When I woke up last night and couldn't sleep, I started reading more of the diary. There was one day in July when Charlotte Rose paid Isabel a visit, which might not have been too out of the ordinary since Isabel was engaged to her brother, but then out of nowhere, Thomas showed up on the same day."

Nancy frowned. "But it seems like he was just showing up randomly all the time, right?"

Emma pursed her lips. "Yes, so it could be nothing. But now Charlotte is back in town and leaving suddenly again, right after Thomas has been arrested. I can't really explain it, but I just have this feeling that she's connected somehow."

Nancy sat down at the bar next to Emma, looking over her shoulder as she did so. Jack went from the far corner of the saloon and into the kitchen, giving Emma a wink on the way. Nancy leaned in close.

"I know you're worried about Charlotte, but you really don't have to be. I've never seen Jack like this with anyone. He is really happy with you. Let's look at this diary and see what else it says. Charlotte and Isabel were almost family. They both loved Dakota dearly. I truly don't think that she would have anything to do with Thomas if she knew that he was harming Isabel."

Emma placed a hand on Nancy's arm. She had never seen Nancy so serious. "Thank you," she said.

They turned back to the diary and continued reading. Nothing significant happened in the next few entries. Charlotte did come visit a few days later, so Emma assumed this must be a time when she had been passing through town. She was just about to give up when she got to the next entry.

"Wait!" Emma cried. "I think this might be something. Listen. August first. Charlotte and Thomas both visited again today. I happened to look out the library window and see both of them in the yard. I opened the window and leaned over the ledge as close as possible without falling out or running the risk of them seeing me. I couldn't make out everything they said, but heard them talking about gold and a few places in town that were for sale. It sounded like they were trying to work out some kind of business deal. Dakota's name was mentioned a few times. I'll have to pay close attention from now on."

Emma sat back and looked at Nancy.

"Wow," Nancy said. "Do you think that no one truly realized how shady Thomas was?"

"I'm not sure," Emma said. "But why would they mention Dakota and the gold and the vacant properties? And if they happened to show up at the same time to visit Isabel, why are they walking around outside talking by themselves?"

Nancy shook her head. "I don't know, but it doesn't look good. At first I thought you were grasping at straws, but now you could really be on to something."

Jack walked back through the kitchen door, whistling and carrying the remains of a basket of apples and carrots that he had just fed to the horses. He looked at the girls sitting at the bar and stopped in his tracks. "What's wrong?" he asked.

Emma quietly closed the diary. "Nothing," she said, a little too cheerfully. "How about we take the horses for a ride today and see what we can find?"

***

The next morning, Emma was the first one in the dining room, and she sat down in what had now become her regular chair. The others soon filed in, and Emma forgot about the diary for a brief moment as she began talking to Jack and bringing everyone up to date on their horseback riding adventure yesterday. Although they had found nothing of substance the day before, it had been nice to get out of town and away from the mystery that couldn't seem to be solved. Emma heard the front door open and looked around the table. Everyone was here: Ezekial, Sheriff Campbell, Sarah, Nancy, and Jack. Who could that be? Her stomach dropped as she turned to the doorway and saw Charlotte Rose.

She was dressed in an elegant dark purple dress, with flowy layers and a black lace overlay. Her dark hair cascaded over her shoulders, and her dark eyes were lined with coal. What would look like an average outfit on anyone else made her look elegant and exotic, and Emma once again found herself examining her dress and smoothing her hair in Charlotte's presence.

It was obvious from the way Charlotte stood in the doorway that she didn't intend to sit and eat, and an awkward silence descended upon the dining room as everyone waited to see why she was just standing there. A single tear escaped from Charlotte's right eye, and Sarah jumped up with her handkerchief to tend to her, as she began to sniffle dramatically and look around.

"What is it?" Sarah asked, ever the motherly type.

"I'm leaving today, and I'll probably never be back," Charlotte answered.

The group at the table looked at each other, everyone waiting for someone else to make sense of what Charlotte was saying. She looked at the entire dining room, then said, "Jack and Emma, can I speak to you in the parlor, please?"

Emma looked at Jack, who was looking back at her with just as much confusion. The two got up and followed Charlotte to the parlor, where she made a sweeping gesture at the couch, imploring them to sit down. Emma perched on the edge of her seat, feeling unsure about herself and what this was about. Jack sat next to her, and Charlotte sat in the armchair across from them.

Charlotte drew in one shaky breath, then exhaled. "I need to tell you something," she began.

Jack and Emma nodded slowly, waiting for her to continue.

She opened her mouth to speak, then faltered. "I think I've done something very bad," she said. "I had no idea how awful Thomas truly was."

Emma's hand flew to her mouth, and she looked at Jack. He looked back at her, with eyes that seemed to show just as much confusion as she felt.

When neither of them responded, Charlotte continued. "I had no idea how corrupt he was. I really thought I was investing my gold wisely, and I thought Isabel was becoming delirious from being shut up in the house for so long."

"What are you saying?" Emma asked slowly.

Charlotte sniffed again, then sat up straighter in her chair. "I'm saying that I helped hide Isabel's gold. I thought Thomas had her best interests in mind. So, when he approached me about hiding the gold in a new location, I thought was trying to help her. He seemed genuinely concerned that she had slipped into a state of depression, but it turns out he didn't actually know where the gold was; he just knew it existed. I helped him hide the gold, and now it's gone."

Chapter 13: Thwarting Thomas's Plans

Emma looked at Jack. This might explain the hidden items in the cave and the sounds Isabel kept hearing from the cellar. Was there really a way that Charlotte could have been working with Thomas? Could she really not have seen how evil he was?

"I don't understand," Emma said. "How did you end up helping Thomas?"

Charlotte sniffled and wiped her eyes with the handkerchief Sarah had given her. "I went to visit Isabel one day. I'd just gotten into town and was riding leisurely up the hill on my horse when I heard galloping behind me. It startled me, and when I turned around in my saddle, I saw Thomas riding towards me. He caught up and we dismounted our horses together and took them to the stable. He told me he was afraid Isabel was going crazy in the house alone, and that she kept misplacing the gold coins and was getting sick."

Emma looked at Jack, then back at Charlotte. "Sick how?"

Charlotte shrugged. "He was very vague about it, but when I went inside, it seemed like she wasn't her usual self. She kept talking about how she was sleeping all the time and feeling ill, getting these headaches and stuff. She talked about Thomas, but it made no sense, and she mentioned the word 'recess' several times. Like the recess in the bookcase wall, I'm assuming?"

Emma nodded, encouraging Charlotte to continue.

"So, after we had visited with her for a while, I thought maybe Thomas was right. The next time I saw him, I agreed to help hide the gold coins, under the premise that he was hiding them for her safekeeping."

"Did she mention chocolate at all?" Jack asked. "In her diary she keeps writing about these chocolates that Thomas brings her, and then it seems like after she eats them, she gets headaches or feels sick or sleeps for a long time."

Charlotte pursed her lips in thought. "Now that I think about it, there was an opened package of chocolates on the table next to the couch. I remember it because her library was kind of messy, which is not like her at all. There were teacups and saucers sitting on the desk, a few books and papers on the end tables, and a blanket on the couch. She's usually so particular about the house, especially the library. That's what made me think she really wasn't doing well." Her eyes grew wide. "Do you think he was poisoning her? With the chocolates?"

Emma and Jack looked at each other.

Emma nodded slowly. "Yes, we suspect that. There are a lot of loose ends we need to tie together."

She was uncertain how much she really wanted to tell Charlotte. She seemed genuinely remorseful about her collaboration with Thomas, but Emma still wasn't sure if she could be trusted.

"Thank you for telling us," Emma said. She turned to Jack. "What about the former store owners? Do you think any of them would be willing to testify against him?"

Jack perked up, looking thoughtfully out the window. "I think it's worth a try. Thomas may have put them out of business, but he did it illegally. If we can get enough people together, we might be able to accomplish something."

Charlotte stood up. "I was planning on leaving today, but I can stay and help spread the word if you want."

"I think that's an excellent idea," Jack said, standing and pulling Emma to her feet. "We'll spread the word. Let's have an informal meeting tonight, at the saloon at seven o'clock."

"Okay, see you then," Charlotte called, already moving to the door.

Emma and Jack went back to the dining room to inform the others, then set out on the town to rustle up anyone they could find.

***

By evening time, Emma felt a great sense of satisfaction at the work they'd done that day. They were able to gather quite a few people who had been put out of business, or whose businesses were suffering because of Thomas's shady deals. By 6:45pm, the saloon was packed with everyone whom Jack and Emma had spoken with that day, as well as some others who had joined from the next town over. The barber, the blacksmith, and the feed store owner had all brought documents that showed how Thomas had completed some shady dealings with them, and many people were talking excitedly, rejuvenated by the idea of finally getting some justice for their unfair treatment.

At exactly seven o'clock, Jack stood at the bar and rapped on a glass with a spoon.

"Attention, please! Attention!" He called.

Emma looked up at him from her seat in front of the room and gave him a reassuring smile.

"As you know, we have called you all here today so that we can collect evidence on Thomas and prove that he has single-handedly ruined this town, and the livelihoods of many. If you have documented proof, please see Sheriff Campbell at the back table." Jack pointed toward the back of the room, and the sheriff waved his hand.

Jack continued. "If you have statements you would like to make regarding the character of Thomas Benson, please see Emma or Charlotte at the front of the room." Jack pointed to the ladies sitting at the table, who both waved at the people, pens poised in hands.

"Okay, we will reconvene in an hour and see what our plan of action is," Jack concluded.

The dining area of the saloon was a flurry of people as everyone rose from their seats and made their way to their respective spots. The room was a buzz of conversation, some lively as long-lost companions were reunited, some loud and abrasive-sounding as others compared their stories.

Emma and Charlotte worked diligently, taking notes as they listened to everyone's complaints. Sheriff Campbell checked over the documents that were brought to him. Finally, Jack called the time, and everyone returned to their seats.

"Thank you, everyone!" Jack said, addressing the crowd.

He was met with a round of applause. When it quieted down, Jack spoke again. "I'd like to propose that we confront Thomas. I think we have enough evidence and enough manpower to show him that we're not afraid of him."

There was a murmur in the audience, and Jack paused to let everyone calm down.

"I propose we bring Thomas here tomorrow to show him the evidence we have against him. If we all stand together, he has no chance. We need to show him that we are smarter than he thinks we are."

Jack let everyone talk amongst themselves for a few seconds so the idea could sink in. He glanced at Emma and shrugged.

"No one has really disagreed with you," she said, looking around.

"Okay!" Jack called again, tapping the glass with the spoon. "Let's form a plan. I'll invite Thomas here, to the saloon, tomorrow night at eight o'clock. You should all be here at seven, and we'll try to talk to him rationally. If we invite him here instead of bombarding him at his office, he'll be on our territory, so to speak, and not his own."

Several murmurs of agreement went through the crowd.

"See you all tomorrow!" Jack called.

To Emma's amazement, no one actually left the saloon. Two groups of people pushed their tables together, many of the men requested glasses of whiskey or beer, and before long, she and Charlotte had jumped in to help Nancy serve everyone.

At one point when Emma was rushing past Jack with another tray of beer for a table, he stopped her, put his arm around her shoulders and whispered in her ear, "After tonight, we just might have enough money to pay those back taxes."

Emma smiled and pecked him on the cheek.

The impromptu party went well into the evening, and everyone stumbled home happy, full, and rejuvenated by the thought of confronting Thomas the next day.

The following morning dragged for Emma. She spent most of the day in the saloon, helping Nancy and Jack tidy up before the group was scheduled to arrive that evening. Jack left midmorning to invite Thomas to the meeting. Without enough evidence, Sheriff Campbell had no choice but to release him from jail. Emma fretted the entire hour that Jack was gone. There were so many things that could go wrong—Thomas may not agree to come, or even worse, he and his goons could hurt Jack. When Jack finally arrived back at the saloon with a smile on his face, Emma knew the plan was still on before he could even say anything.

Morning turned to afternoon, afternoon turned to early evening, and finally, the former business owners and townspeople began filing in, even earlier than expected. Emma found herself once again helping Nancy in the kitchen and running food and drinks out to the tables. As the eight o'clock hour loomed near, an eerie hush fell upon the saloon.

At eight o'clock sharp, the saloon door burst open, and Thomas Benson's large frame filled the door, flanked by his henchmen. He stopped short at the sight of the entire saloon filled with people, all of whom he had screwed over in some way. The sneer on his face faded as he took in the full room, the tables of paying customers, and the people whom he thought he had driven out of town.

He took a step back, but Jack and Sheriff Campbell rushed to the door.

"Oh no," Jack said, gesturing to a table near the front of the door. "Have a seat."

Thomas, still dumbfounded, sat down, and looked like he was in a daze. He gestured wildly at his buddies, and they sat down next to him.

"We've called this meeting today," Jack began, "because we have evidence to show that you have cheated people out of money, evicted people illegally, and committed other crimes."

Thomas stood up so fast that his chair fell over behind him. "You have no proof!" he yelled.

"But we do," Emma chimed in, rushing to Jack's side. "Everyone in here either has illegal eviction notices from you, false receipts, or delayed shipment notices, which caused them to go out of business. We also have reason to believe you stole gold from Isabel."

Emma caught Thomas's henchmen looking at each other out of the corner of her eye. She wondered if even they knew he was in over his head.

Thomas turned as if to dart towards the door, but Sheriff Campbell and a large man wearing overalls and wielding a pickaxe were faster and blocked the door. Several men throughout the saloon rose from their tables, until one by one, everyone had stood up. Sheriff Campbell motioned to the table where he had been sitting, pointing to the folder of documents that were on top. Charlotte brought the documents over and placed the folder in front of Thomas. Emma brought the written statements she had collected and placed them near the folder.

A hush fell over the room. Tension filled the air as everyone watched Thomas, who seemingly could find nothing to say.

"What is this?" Thomas finally asked.

"This is the evidence we just mentioned," Jack said. "You could not possibly have thought you would get away with this forever, did you?"

Thomas said nothing as he sifted through the documents and statements. Emma looked at Jack, who looked back smugly at her. They had him. Sheriff Campbell looked at Jack, then nodded and walked over to Thomas.

"You are hereby under arrest for falsifying documents, bribery and corruption, and theft."

Sheriff Campbell placed his hand on Thomas's arm and helped him stand up. It was completely silent as everyone in the saloon watched Sheriff Campbell put the handcuffs on Thomas and lead him away, his head hung in shame.

Chapter 14: Embracing Love and Mysteries of the Past

It was late by the time the saloon closed. After Sheriff Campbell lead Thomas away, his men left as well. There was much discussion as to whether they would be charged as accessories to the crimes. After more celebratory drinks and much camaraderie, one by one, the townspeople began to leave, each grateful that justice would be done.

Sarah thanked Emma and Jack when she went back to the inn because for the first time in as long as she could remember, all the rooms were full for the evening. Ezekial thanked Emma and Jack because he was happy that he was able to use his meticulous note-taking collection. Nancy was happy that the saloon had been busier than it ever had, giving her the opportunity to earn more money.

Emma stacked the last glass behind the bar and looked outside. It was a comfort to see lights on at the inn on every floor. She was gazing out the window when Jack came up behind her.

"What are you looking at?" he asked.

"Look at the inn," Emma said, gesturing out the window. "Isn't it neat to see all the lights on? When do you think the last time is that the inn has been completely full for the night?"

Jack smiled. "I'm not sure I ever remember a time when all the lights were on. This is usually not a town where people stop for more than a few hours." He playfully swatted her with a towel. "It's sure a good thing you did."

Emma laughed. "I only stopped because I had to." She turned to face Jack, and he leaned in to give her a sweet, slow kiss.

"I'm really glad your stagecoach broke down," he said.

"So am I," Emma agreed.

An awkward silence descended between them. Jack took a step back and shuffled his feet. "Well, it seems like the part for your stagecoach will be in any day, and I know you were excited about this new job you were going across the county for...." Jack's voice trailed off.

Emma patiently waited for him to continue. She hoped that he was going to ask her what she thought he was going to ask her.

"What do you think about staying here?"

Emma smiled. "Really?"

Jack cleared his throat. "Yes. I know you have only been here a short amount of time, but I'm falling totally head over heels for you. I love your laugh, I love your smile, and I love your sharp wit. And I think you're beautiful."

Emma's cheeks were burning from smiling so much. She looked up at Jack and was sure that he could see the answer in her face before she even replied. "Oh Jack, I'm so happy to hear that you feel the same way that I do. I've enjoyed every minute with you. I'm falling for you too, and I was hoping you'd ask me to stay here."

Jack smiled at her again. "You feel the same way I do? You think I'm beautiful?" he asked jokingly.

Emma smiled as she stepped into his embrace. "Something like that."

"Come on," Jack said. "I'll walk you to the inn."

They made their way out to the street, and sauntered slowly down the sidewalk as they discussed the future.

"I feel like it was fate that your stagecoach broke down," Jack said. "What are the odds that you would stop here, in this little ghost town?"

Emma smiled. "When I was riding along, I was getting so tired. I told myself I'd stop at the next town, but when I got here, I briefly considered going one town farther. I didn't think there was anything or anyone left."

Jack looked up and down the street before responding. "What do you think about moving on, maybe to the next town? I think if we went to a different city, even the next bigger town, you would have a chance at another investigative journalism job. Maybe I could legitimately sell the saloon and open a new place."

Emma rolled that thought around in her head. She hadn't given much thought to what being with Jack might mean. She had assumed they'd just stay here. The saloon had been in his family for a while, and he'd lived here for years. Yet what was there for her to do here? She and Jack had solved the mystery. She would have nothing else to do with her time now that their little detective work was done.

She looked at Jack. "I think you might be right," she said slowly. "If you're ready to move on, then I am too. It's hard to imagine that the town has much of a future. Maybe it would be better to start fresh somewhere else."

Jack nodded. "I'm so happy you stopped here, but I never expected you to want to stay here. From the first time I looked at you, I could see the fire in your eyes that was too great for this has-been town. If you'll agree to go with me, I'll start the process of selling the saloon tomorrow."

Emma took one long look up and down the street. She couldn't imagine living permanently in a place like this. The town was quaint and nostalgic, but it was not where she belonged. She squeezed Jack's hand tight.

"I'll be happy wherever you are, Jack, but if it were up to me, then yes, we would not stay here," she stated.

They had reached the front porch of the inn, and as it was well after midnight, she fully expected everyone who was staying there to be asleep, and was surprised to walk through the front door and hear people in the parlor and the dining room. She grabbed Jack's hand and pulled him down the hallway to the parlor, where everyone stood to cheer when the two entered.

Emma dropped Jack's hand as she looked around the room in shock. The guests of the inn were still up, many of them drinking coffee or beer and chatting with each other. Several people came forward to thank Jack and Emma once again and to congratulate Jack on his successful business day at the saloon. Jack introduced Emma to many formerly successful farmers and businessmen, along with several of their families. Emma found herself talking to many of the women, who were all impressed by her investigative journalism stories. Most of the women had never strayed far from the ghost town, so they were enthralled with her stories of travel and adventure.

By the time everyone retired to their own rooms, Emma was exhausted. She trudged up the stairs, trailing her hand along the banister as she went. She fell into bed without washing her face or hanging up her dress that lay discarded on the chair in the corner.

She awoke to bright sunlight streaming through the window and knew immediately that she'd missed breakfast. She thought of all the people she had talked to the night before and how welcoming everyone had been. What would it be like if she and Jack stayed in the town and tried to help rebuild it? There was much work to be done, and maybe it wasn't even possible to completely turn around a ghost town. But the citizens were still enthusiastic, and everyone was eager to help each other. They did have a town Sheriff and several operable businesses still. Was it worth a shot? Deep in thought, she descended the stairs and headed to the saloon, where Jack was taking inventory.

"Good morning," she called as she opened the door.

Jack looked up from his papers and smiled at her. Emma felt butterflies in her stomach as he crossed the room to greet her.

"Hi," he said, giving her a kiss.

"I can't believe I slept this long," Emma said, pulling up a stool at the bar.

"I could barely sleep last night," Jack said. "I kept replaying everything over in my mind."

"I've been thinking a lot about what we talked about yesterday," Emma began slowly.

Jack set his papers on top of the bar and looked at her, an expression of concern on his face.

Emma took a deep breath and blurted out her thoughts. "What do you think about staying here?"

Jack's shoulders relaxed and he leaned forward, placing both hands on the counter.

"Yes," Emma said. "I've been thinking about this all morning. After talking to the women in the parlor last night and seeing everyone come together in the saloon the past two days to work with us, I think the spirit of the town is still here."

She looked at Jack, wondering if she sounded ridiculous. Just yesterday they had agreed to leave the town and start somewhere new.

"I do wonder what could happen now that everyone has come together," Jack said. "The saloon could be a thriving business again. You could start a newspaper here. If we have paying customers and citizens again, the town could be what it once was."

"I think we owe it to ourselves to stay here and see," Emma said. "This town brought us together. We can't abandon it now."

Chapter 15: The End

"Order! Order!" The judge banged the gavel on the bench and waited for the buzz in the courtroom to quiet down.

Emma took a quick look around. She and Jack were in the front of the courtroom, waiting to be called to the stand as the next witnesses. In the rows behind them sat Nancy, Ezekial, Sarah, and Charlotte, along with many of the townspeople. Several of the men had come straight from the fields, their overalls dusty from planting crops in an effort to rejuvenate the town. The mason sat next to one of the draftsmen, and Emma had heard them talking during one of the breaks about their plans for future construction and additions that would be needed on several buildings.

Emma looked at the judge, waiting for him to continue. He banged his gavel one last time and the whispers were silenced.

She stood with her hand on the back of the bench in front of her, poised and ready to walk to the front. In her other hand, she clutched the diary. Her palms were sweaty, and she had to wipe them alternately on her dress. The judge called her to the witness stand, and Jack gave her free hand a squeeze as she shimmied her way out of the row and up to the front.

Emma took a shaky breath as everyone watched her walk to the front of the room. She told the story of finding the diary in her room at the inn, the clues that led her and Jack to the mansion to find the hidden spot in the bookshelf where the gold was no longer hidden, and the testimonies they had gathered from the townspeople.

Jack was called to the stand, and eventually so was Sheriff Campbell, who testified that he had not sanctioned many of the evictions. The hours went by, and finally the court adjourned for lunch.

Jack, Emma, and Charlotte left the courtroom and gathered outside city hall.

"I just know I'll be called next," Charlotte said. "I don't know why, but I'm nervous. Thomas is glaring at everyone who testifies against him. He's terrifying."

"He can't do anything though," Emma said. He's surrounded by Sheriff Campbell and other officers, not to mention everyone he's wronged who's here to watch the trial. Nothing will happen to you."

Charlotte smiled nervously. "You're right. Thank you."

One by one, everyone started filing back into the courtroom. The judge took his seat and had to bang his gavel only once for attention. Charlotte was the first one called to the stand, and she made her way to the front of the courtroom with a nervous glance at Emma and Jack.

The judge asked her about her relationship with Thomas and her connection to Dakota, the gold, and Isabel. Charlotte began to tell her story about believing that Isabel was unwell. The judge listened, and the prosecutor asked several questions about the gold and where it was hidden. She began to tear up after being asked the same question in multiple different ways.

She sniffled, then gave her answer. "I already told you: the gold was hidden in a recess in the wall. That's how I knew where to look. Isabel kept talking about the recess. It was somehow connected to Thomas."

At the word "recess," Ezekial and Sarah began whispering frantically together in the courtroom. Ezekial leaned forward and tapped the lawyer who was representing Onyx Falls.

The judge banged his gavel again. "Order!" he called.

"Your honor, we have one more witness," the lawyer said.

The judge sighed, and the lawyer called Sarah to the stand.

After introducing herself and describing her role in the community, as well as how Thomas's shady business dealings brought financial ruin to her hotel, she was able to present her evidence.

"About the same time Isabel disappeared, there was a male guest in my hotel. I remember this because I don't often have too many men who stay by themselves. I occasionally get businessmen passing through

town, but even that has been rare. This man was by himself, and he
stayed for a short period of time. When he first arrived, he used the
word 'recess.' He said he was in town to do some business with Thomas
Benson but was vague about what he was here for. He said Thomas was
going on recess and he would be here to quote, 'handle business.'" Sarah
raised both hands in the air and motioned with her fingers as she said
the word quote.

There was a twitter in the audience, and the judge banged his gavel
to silence everyone.

Emma and Charlotte leaned toward each other with a knowing
look. Charlotte's hand flew to her mouth, and she cried out, "A recess!
Like a trip! This whole time I thought she was talking about the space
in the wall. She knew Thomas was taking her on a trip! A trip she never
came back from!"

"Silence!" bellowed the judge.

The courtroom grew silent.

Emma looked over at Thomas, who was slouched lower in his seat,
head lowered, as if he was studying the floor.

"Look," Emma said, elbowing Jack.

Jack looked at Emma and raised his eyebrows.

***

The trial opened the next morning with the cross examination of
Sarah, who continued to relay the events in her soft, soothing voice.

After all the witnesses were questioned and the evidence was
brought against Thomas, the jury dismissed to deliberate.

Emma sat in the courtroom waiting, her knee bobbing up and
down. She couldn't believe the trial was taking this long. Finally, the
jury came back, and the judge called the court to order. The verdict
was read aloud. Thomas was charged with kidnapping, theft, falsifying
documents, plus a slew of other crimes. As he was handcuffed and

taken from the courtroom, he called out, "Isabel is hidden at my house! She's alive! I didn't kill her!"

Emma turned to Jack, then to Sarah. Nancy turned to Ezekial. Charlotte was already out the door before anyone could stop her.

Emma and Jack raced after Charlotte, following her through the back streets of town until they came to a modest house on a narrow street. By the time they reached the house, Charlotte was halfway up the steps of the front porch, yelling for Isabel.

When she got no answer, she picked up a rock and heaved it through the front window, sending shards of glass scattering in all directions. She carefully reached through the window and unlocked the door, leaving it wide open for Emma and Jack to follow through. They ran up the steps, yelling for Isabel. A thumping sound and a muffled cry came from upstairs, and the three tore down the hall and raced toward the noise. Charlotte rattled the doorknob, but the door was locked.

"Isabel!" She called, rattling the doorknob, and knocking on the door. "It's me, Charlotte. Are you in here?"

A muffled voice came from inside. "Help!"

"Stand back!" Jack called. "I'm breaking the door down!"

Jack charged at the door, and it splintered from the force of his fist. There in the room was Isabel, tied up but alive, on a small couch.

Charlotte rushed across the room and threw her arms around Isabel, quickly untying her.

While the two women had a tearful reunion, Emma went to the window to look out. If there was an escape out of this room, why hadn't Isabel taken it? She looked out the window, then down at the ground. There was a fenced-in area below the window with a field of wild boars, roaming around in search of their next bite of food.

Two days later, Emma once again found herself in the saloon, helping Nancy bring drinks to tables.

"Can you believe this?" Emma asked, gesturing toward the full dining room area.

Nancy stopped stacking the glasses behind the bar and looked out, smiling. "It's amazing," she said. "I don't think I've ever seen the bar this full and lively."

"I'm so glad you stuck around, even though the majority of the people in this town already started to leave," Emma said, then burst out laughing. "And without your muffins, this case may never have been solved."

Nancy let out a giggle, then hung her head. "Cooking has never been my specialty," she said. "But I'm glad my muffins were finally put to some kind of use."

Emma continued. "Your sense of humor really got me through some of these days. Everything seemed so bleak for a while."

Nancy's smile grew wider as she looked at Emma. "I'm so glad to hear that. As a kid, my parents were always telling me to be seen and not heard, so I grew up trying to suppress my personality. I'm glad it's finally become useful."

"I wouldn't have it any other way," Emma chuckled.

Jack came over to the bar and tapped a spoon on a glass and called for silence.

"Attention!" He called.

The dining room quieted down, and everyone turned to face Jack. Emma looked out at the room and saw Sheriff Campbell sitting with Thomas's former henchmen, who had agreed to work with him as law enforcement officers in training. Sarah, Isabel, and Charlotte were sitting together at another table, and Ezekial was at a third table, looking at files with one of the men who had been selected for jury duty at the trial.

"Thank you all for coming to our celebration tonight," Jack began. He looked back and winked at Emma. "Onyx Falls is well on its way to revival, all thanks to this wonderful lady right here."

The dining room erupted in applause, and Jack extended his hand toward Emma, who walked around the bar to stand next to him. She surveyed the room, smiling at everyone she had gotten to know. She waved to a few people in the back of the room whom she had not gotten to say hi to yet. The applause was still going when Emma looked back at Jack, who was just lowering himself to one knee.

If you enjoyed this book, please take a few moments to write a review of it. Thank you!

Milton Keynes UK
Ingram Content Group UK Ltd.
UKHW042310160224
437951UK00004B/371

9 798224 655342

Gallery Books
Editor: Peter Fallon

POEMS
Patrick MacDonogh

Patrick MacDonogh

POEMS

Edited and introduced by
Derek Mahon

Gallery Books

Poems
is first published
simultaneously in paperback
and in a clothbound edition
on 28 June 2001.

The Gallery Press
Loughcrew
Oldcastle
County Meath
Ireland

*All rights reserved. For permission
to reprint or broadcast these poems
write to The Gallery Press.*

Introduction © Derek Mahon 2001
Poems and frontispiece © The Estate
  of Patrick MacDonogh 2001

ISBN 1 85235 287 6 (*paperback*)
     1 85235 288 4 (*clothbound*)

The Gallery Press acknowledges the financial assistance
of An Chomhairle Ealaíon / The Arts Council, Ireland,
and the Arts Council of Northern Ireland.

Contents

Introduction

Patrick MacDonogh (1902-1961), a contemporary of MacNeice and Kavanagh but, unlike them, out of print for a generation, published five collections of poems between 1927 and 1958 and was highly regarded during his lifetime, with a modest international reputation based on a handful of recurrent anthology choices. Not an immensely prolific output and, despite what amounts to a cult following, he has recently seemed in danger of slipping through the cracks of literary history, which is one of the reasons he needs to be re-issued. He is also a very fine poet indeed, which is its own argument. The five collections were: *Flirtation* (G. F. Healy, Dublin, 1927), *A Leaf in the Wind* (Quota Press, Belfast, 1929), *The Vestal Fire* (Orwell Press, Dublin, 1941), *Over the Water* (Orwell Press, 1943) and *One Landscape Still and Other Poems* (Secker & Warburg, London, 1958) — a distinguished though not extensive body of work, one rendered even more exiguous by a self-critical severity which led him to discard, select and refine from volume to volume until, with the Secker collection, he arrived at an almost final text.

The contents of the present volume are based on that collection, while dropping eleven and adding eight, including six 'new' poems from MacDonogh's brief final period, 1957-61. The Secker book, though relatively slim, was in effect a collected poems, 'all that he wished to preserve' arranged according to his own idea of his work, an order (not necessarily chronological) followed here. Eight poems are collected here for the first time. 'Afterpeace', 'The Dream' and 'Marriage Song' first appeared in *The Dublin Magazine*, 'The Rust is on the Lilac Bloom' and 'Far from Ben Bulben' in *The Irish Times*; while the other three are reproduced from his own typescripts. He dedicated the Secker volume to his wife, the late Ellen May ('Maisie') Connell MacDonogh; in the same spirit, this re-issue of his work is dedicated to his two daughters, Caroline and Boyer. Boyer is an artist and lives in County Waterford. Caroline, a writer who lives in France and teaches at Caen University, is our principal source of biographical information, and her as yet unpublished doctoral thesis, 'A Study of Patrick MacDonogh's Poetry', has been invaluable in elucidating background and theme. She concedes that *One Landscape Still* was an ambiguous title. MacDonogh was not saying, 'Ireland is the only place for me,' but something more like, 'Here we are, prisoners of our condition'; though it may also refer to some idea of the eternal, 'the resurrection of the body and the life to come'.

That volume, long out of print and now a collector's item, is a decent period piece bound and wrapped in quiet greens, the dustjacket proclaiming it a 'Poetry Book Society Recommendation' and recommending 'other poets from our [Secker's] list' including Theodore Roethke, Burns Singer, D. J. Enright and Jonathan Griffin. The front flyleaf informs us that MacDonogh first made his appearance on their list in 1944, in the small anthology *Irish Poems of Today* selected by Geoffrey Taylor from contributions to *The Bell*. This, it continues, is 'the first collection of his poems to be published and they reflect the author's passionate love of his native land.' The given price was 12/6d net. But of course it was by no means his first collection to be published, though his first (and last) to be published in England. As for 'passionate love of his native land', the ambiguous title has misled the blurb-writer, for there's rather more to it than that: '*tormented* love', not unique to him, would be more like it — though torment is passion too. The book was reviewed in a respectful if subdued fashion by, among others, John Hewitt (*Threshold*) and John Montague (*Studies*). Hewitt provided a brisk summary of MacDonogh's progress from the early poems with their conventional properties of willows, roses, lilacs, Babylon, Nineveh, Troy and, 'touching a forelock to local circumstance', leprechauns. He remarked on a Dowsonian atmosphere and Yeatsian derivation, noted an absence of originality but recognized the 'literary good breeding'. Serious praise he reserved for later work, especially 'Escape to Love' and 'O, Come to the Land!', where he found in MacDonogh 'a hard objectivity towards himself and his generation'; and he concluded by recommending him as 'an addition to our imaginative estate'. Montague acknowledged 'the much anthologized lyrics, graceful and plaintive as early Yeats', where 'romantic lyrical pain merges into dialect and folk poems', but noticed the 'brooding, obsessive nature' of the book, and the 'desolate divisions of the spirit' they describe. Both remark on the Yeatsian properties and cadences — though even Yeats, of course, borrowed from Nora Hopper and Frank O'Connor, to name but two; equally both Hewitt and Montague were aware of something new and different. Somewhat belatedly, MacDonogh had established himself as a distinctive voice.

He was born in Dublin, where his father was founder and headmaster of Avoca School, Blackrock, and educated there and at Trinity College, where he read for an arts degree, shone at athletics and subsequently took a Ph.D. with a thesis on Allingham. After graduation he worked as a teacher and commercial artist before joining the staff of Arthur Guinness Son and Company, where he later held a senior executive post. The background is important. One of five children, he grew up in an earnest and convivial Protestant middle-class environment of tennis parties and hockey sticks, subsequently playing hockey for Ireland: a privileged environment also characteristic of his active and linear professional career, especially the prime-of-life years when he and his family lived at Cintra, a pleasant Georgian country house near Kinsealy, north County Dublin. Rod and gun, field and stream, featured at weekends; the artist and novelist Ralph Cusack was a neighbour. During his last years, when ill health obliged him to take early retirement, MacDonogh lived in 'reduced circumstances' at Malahide and Portmarnock. Both he and his wife, a well-known mezzo-soprano, broadcast frequently on Radio Éireann, she specializing in Schubert, he in sporting and literary matters. Hill walker, fly-fisherman, golfer etc, he knew the country intimately from Wicklow to Mayo, from Antrim to Cork; but the customary landscapes of his poetry are those of north and south County Dublin, and of County Meath. After a certain point they are even more specifically those of the Kinsealy woodlands and the Malahide estuary. His friends included Lord Moyne, 'Con' Leventhal and Séamus Kelly ('Quidnunc' of *The Irish Times*); in England, Betjeman and Laurie Lee, the author of *Cider with Rosie*. He drove fast cars, Sunbeam Talbot and Jaguar, co-founded the Galway Oyster Festival, took a hand in John Huston's Youghal production of *Moby Dick*, and made frequent appearances in literary pubs like the Pearl Bar and the Red Bank. Brian Fallon, in *An Age of Innocence: Irish Culture 1930-1960*, tells us this 'sensitive, much-loved man' was one of the *Dublin Magazine* inner circle. He contributed also, as his acknowledgements indicate, to the books pages of large-circulation newspapers like *The Observer*, and to New York magazines including *Harper's* and *The American Mercury*.

Flirtation was interesting less for the poems than for the black-and-white cover drawing (his own) in what Brian Fallon calls 'the then fashionable Harry Clarke style', the style also of Cecil ffrench-Salkeld's decorative murals in Davy Byrne's (Dublin) pub: an art-deco 1920s-Arcadian idiom depicting harlequinesque *fêtes galantes*. (Celtic motifs would appear later.) We associate these properties with the whimsical, adolescent nostalgia of Laforgue and *Le Grand Meaulnes*; and indeed there was, and remained, something lost-domainish about MacDonogh's sensibility — an inflection audible even now in the work of William Trevor and Jennifer Johnston. These early poems are juvenilia, Keatsian pastiche; though later developments suggest that 'The Eve of St Agnes' remained a useful and even bracing model. It's not until *A Leaf in the Wind* that he begins to be interesting, with 'Helen' and 'A Drunk Man' (later 'The Drunkard'), which made it into the Secker volume. Not included in that volume is the unusual and rather rambling 'A Belfast Shipping Clerk Goes to His Work', where a young MacDonogh figure, sent by Guinness's to the northern capital, with its 'gantries looming through the mist', thinks fondly of summers in Wicklow, 'the quiet crackling of the gorse' and 'the shining altar of the sea'.

The Vestal Fire is a heroic epithalamion in thirteen sections, some long, some short. A devoted lover of 'companionable women', almost a Muse poet in the Gravesian sense, he embraced sexual love as the highest form of human understanding, and these fourteen pages, intensely erotic yet idealistic — even 'Petrarchan', as he says elsewhere — are his first sustained attempt to measure his own experience of this not uncommon revelation. It's a love poem, or series of love poems, in search of absolute sincerity and commitment, almost of self-definition — 'my constant light' — where the winsome, wanly dancing nymph-like figure of the *Flirtation* cover girl is found to be a grown-up woman and treated accordingly. An excited and slightly incoherent work, over-long, overly discursive, overly cerebral, it's also overly anxious to arrive at the right sort of conclusions. But the short passages he retained and which are included here ('Curtain' and 'You, Too, at Midnight Suddenly Awaking') are very fine; and the exercise, noble in itself, allowed him to approach a subject more fully developed later — that of essential solitude. Here already, in this solemnly happy poem with its echoes of Spenser and Donne ('This night is ours'), an austere, quasi-religious disposition makes itself heard, one oddly nostalgic for a spiritual regimen it rejects too violently. The positive, 'life-loving' aspirations the poem so vigorously espouses co-exist with an exile among 'waking thoughts' under an 'actual cold observant sky'. It's the old mind-body problem, with 'dancing spring' cursed by a need 'to discipline my thought with naked line'.

Over the Water, published only two years later, is the culmination of his early work and remains a remarkable achievement by any standards. Here, collected for the first time, are the classic anthology pieces, the popular lyrics and several intriguing, much more 'modern' poems like 'Dodona's Oaks were Still' and the title piece itself. He is no longer writing tentative poems; nearly all will survive later inspection, and most are included here. How to explain this sudden burst of creative confidence and exactitude? An emotional settling, perhaps, with wife and family, and a new political awareness after a long silence during the 1930s — an awareness not quite explicit in the manner of Auden and

MacNeice, but implicit in the situations of his 'characters', released from tedium and galvanized into fruitful tension and flow by the wartime atmosphere both in Ireland and England. Brian Inglis, the author of *West Briton* (1962), once explained that, on the outbreak of the Second World War, he and his Malahide set joined the British armed forces 'as a matter of course' — though with the secret proviso, in his own case, that he would resign his RAF commission should Britain offer to re-invade 'Éire'. MacDonogh, older but from a not dissimilar social group, must have had similarly complex feelings about the whole business, especially in the light of his friendship with the English poet Phoebe Hesketh, the 'war widow' in the poem of that title. But the wartime mood affected him in another way too, confirming a cultural identification with the Gael and issuing in the 'folk' poems for which he became chiefly known, 'She Walked Unaware' and 'The Widow of Drynam'.

He writes elsewhere of the Irish poetic genius as 'at once spiritual and sensuous', qualities we associate with, say, Clarke's 'The Straying Student' or Padraic Fallon's 'Mary Hynes', and which he too combines here. These dramatic monologues, rural in setting, their speakers respectively a love-lorn youth and a proud old woman, are beautifully crafted and in some ways characteristic utterances, artifacts even, from the much-maligned Yeats and de Valera era of traditional sanctity and comeliness, which produced so much of the finest Irish art and literature. A centuries-old tradition of *aisling* and *cailleach* lives on in both, together with an unregenerate eroticism and radical defiance. Here are Synge's 'wild words', the garrulous narration, dramatic self-awareness and aristocratic peasant pride, the wandering lines and 'planted' off-rhymes, the concrete imagery and emotional realism of Ó Rathaille and Eibhlín Dhubh Ní Chonaill. If 'Be Still as You Are Beautiful' seems to recommend, shamelessly, that the recipient 'look good and say nothing', the heroic and vital note in 'The Widow of Drynam', as so often in Gaelic poetry, is struck by a woman, in the voice of an Ireland most of us have forgotten or never knew: for one not really familiar with what Jennifer Johnston calls 'my own unspoken language', his re-creation, in a modern setting, of the intonations of the Gaelic eighteenth century is the more remarkable.

Amorous, introspective, philosophical and contemporary-history poems merge into one another with their wonderful titles: 'Soon with the Lilac Fades Another Spring', 'This Morning I Wakened Among Loud Cries of Seagulls'. A love poem will present itself in folk guise, a 'war' poem will contain a love story; everything discursive carries a specific gravity of intense emotional experience, mixing memory and desire. A generalized piece like 'The Bone-Bright Tree', for instance, a codger's lament for 'courteous acumen', 'astringency' and 'strict articulation', invoking the stoical suicide of Petronius, *arbiter elegantiarum*, records one of a series of psychological crises relating, in part, to a vaguely guilt-ridden detachment he seems to have considered endemic to the Protestant situation. This anxiety is present even in the much-quoted Swiftian epigram 'No Mean City', a bleak glimpse of Dublin social life in the not so distant past. Dogged by a morbid sense of isolation, despite job and family, he tried to escape this, in life, through manic activity of various kinds — and, in the work, by embodying the rupture between subject and object, perceiver and perceived, text and context, in highly wrought formal structures. As if this isola-tion were not enough, Caroline, in her thesis, alludes to that Meredithian theme, 'the deep and prolonged struggle between man and wife', quotes Coleridge on 'the unfathomable hell within', and finds here, as in his crisp abstractions, the true strength and modernity of the work.

One of the last in whom a 'Revival' texture and aesthetic are evident, he risked inclusion among the 'twilighters' and 'anti-quarians' to whom his friend Beckett gave such a hard time in the 1934 essay 'Recent Irish Poetry'. The adopted personalities and archaic coloration of the folk poems might seem to incriminate him, together with F. R. Higgins and early Clarke, in 'the flight from self-awareness' and even a yearning for 'the wan bliss at the rim'; but the pathos of these poems springs from a very personal romanticism. The son in 'Drynam' has gone to 'the war', perhaps an older war; but with 'Over the Water' and 'War Widow' we are definitely in the 1940s. These belong to a whole genre of wartime love-and-separation poetry, fiction and film, a genre to which MacNeice and Elizabeth Bowen were only two of the most vivid contributors. 'War Widow' is addressed to Phoebe Hesketh, with whom MacDonogh conducted a fruitful friendship then and later; while the magnificent 'Over the Water', one of his finest achievements, inscribes their relationship in another of his dramatic monologues, though dramatic in a more complex fashion than hitherto. As in 'Drynam', an adopted personality speaks. A soldier, in London during the Blitz, thinks of his lover in Ireland and wishes her beside him: a displacement of the poet, in Ireland, thinking of his lover in England and wishing himself there. A frequent visitor, he knew the London atmosphere, and picks up on the 'apocalyptic' mood of the time: for example, despite obvious differences, he thought highly of the work of Dylan Thomas. There is a comparable exhilaration here, though the sub-text is one of loss, failure, unfulfilment: his final theme, if one redeemed by his gift for clarity of design and aphoristic closure.

Conceived as a birthright, the theme is symbolized in the 'bone-bright tree' (compare and contrast Joyce's 'heaventree of stars'); as a moonlit hieroglyphic landscape void of human agency but alive with creatures, owl and pigeon, mouse and fox, like Leopardi's night-time glade of dancing hares. What is figured is a crisis of sensibility, an examination not of conscience but of consciousness. A morbid unspontaneity — the 'original sin', so to speak, in the Protestant soul — is scrutinized with self-conscious unspontaneity. He doesn't seek, much less achieve, the perhaps rather forced emotional triumphalism of 'A Prayer for My Daughter' and 'Among School Children'. His theme is implenitude; his wistful love of organic growth and generative archetype goes unrequited. The waves break regardless; the trees are mute. This is what happens in 'Dunleary Harbour' and 'Dodona's Oaks were Still'. The first of these, another of his strongest pieces, asks the old question, 'Was it spirit or flesh first committed, first suffered the wrong?' — and adapts a Bowen phrase to commemorate a vitality, his own and that of his social group, now evidently a thing of the past: 'the death of the innocent heart, the end of surprise'. The suburban trees of Dunleary (*sic*) take on, characteristically, a mythic and mystical significance in 'Dodona's Oaks'. According to Graves, the oracular oaks of Dodona in Epirus were the object of a Diana moon-cult, involving mistletoe, therefore sacred to the Muse; but, in the eremitic solitude imagined by the narrator — a St Kevin-at-Glendalough scene — the druidic boughs prove unforthcoming, are silent in wind and limb.

Silent too is the sleeping house in that fine dejection ode, 'Escape to Love', as he wakes to dawn consciousness — 'felicitous space', in Bachelard's phrase, where, taking the fun out of birdsong and sunny window, the mental sky darkens and a premonition of death stirs 'like a mouse in the gut'. (The book about bones and mice in 20th-century poetry has yet to be written.) This is a short story, a sketch for a novel, a spiritual autobiography and diagnosis. On 'the first bright Sunday in March' he walks abroad through 'poisoned lands' and 'sun-dazed' fields, remembering with pain his inhibited mother, her 'frosty duty', 'chilly nurture' and 'acrimonious care': 'Mother of Rimbaud, weep for what you have done!' He contemplates with 'rueful self-knowledge' a limited literary achievement, his spiritual apostasy in 'a long indolent act of sacrilege' and — 'political orphan too' — his suspension between two kinds of sectarianism and estrangement from society generally; then, in a strange and violent conclusion, sacrifices himself to save a hunted hare. (The book about hares in Irish poetry is also long overdue.) There is something both Orphic and Christian about this gratuitous gesture; though its failure, in narrative terms, is of a piece with the existential failure the poem documents. At least we are not dealing here with a flight from self-awareness: *au contraire*, 'Escape' is MacDonogh's most serious and resourceful effort to establish personal and cultural authenticity.

The fairy-tale enchanted castle of earlier work diminishes finally, in 'Far from Ben Bulben' and 'Make Believe', to bone structure, the skull beneath the skin: to his 'proper dark', a bungalow at Portmarnock. Nothing wrong with that, many might envy him; but Caroline finds 'resignation' in the last poems — which she also describes, more positively, as 'succinct' and 'testamentary'. Though sound in wind and limb and evincing, she says, 'a kind of romantic and austere dignity', MacDonogh fell prey to psychiatric problems and spent increasing periods in mental hospitals. One of these coincided with the arrival of the Secker proofs, which he had no opportunity to correct; so that volume, his life's work, is full of misprints. Hand-written corrections appear, fortunately, in copies of the published book and are, of course, incorporated here. Besides the three previously unpublished typescripts, an old Guinness ledger survives where, carefully inscribed in fountain-pen blue ink, he sketches a perfunctory fragment of autobiography dwindling to diary entries and disconsolate reflections on the Cold War: 'If this misery was caused by the pressure of these or similar enormous anxieties it would at least have some dignity and honour about it . . . but as it really springs instead from an incorrigible ignorance of the value of money and from the impotent creative desire of one more emasculated soul I find it merely mean and despicable.' If, with the re-invasion of Ireland and other vulnerable societies by 'global capital', and the resulting devastation, the work of the Revival has to be done again, MacDonogh and others may yet come into their own.

This edition retains his order of contents. The rationale may seem inscrutable, but it is his own mature configuration, his own 'bone-bright tree': he placed the lines in a certain sequence, and the poems too — perhaps on the principle of 'radial time'. We are not trying to construct a contemporary, but granting a dead man the 'ineluctable modality' of his historical period. Nor is this mere antiquarianism; for the poems live. Their knotty cerebrations and serious striving, the half-dozen masterpieces conceived, as it were, in thunderstorms, together with other 'glories infrequent, authentic, vouchsafed though unsought', constitute his own version of 'failing better'. 'To be an artist is to fail as no other dare fail,' says Beckett in the *Dialogues*: 'that failure in his world and the shrink from it desertion, art and craft, good housekeeping.' The idea of failure, much underrated, thrives between freedom and necessity, between gravity and grace, in an 'endless quarrel between earth and sky'. The lonely impulse of delight negotiates with bone structure:

> *One landscape still!* —
> *Memorial acres, old demented trees*
> *About a crumbling house, a stony hill,*
> *A solitary lake — forever these*
> *Restrict the image and impose their will.*

Occupying, says Brian Fallon, 'a middle ground between traditionalism and modernism, as also between the consciously "Irish" note of Higgins and the more cosmopolitan tone of MacNeice, MacDonogh produced a compact and resilient body of work with a distinctive character'. Obsessed with youth and novelty, we sometimes patronize previous generations, imagining them to have been more naive than they were; for, of course, everything has been done or thought before in one form or another, though our historical provincialism tends to ignore the fact. We patronize, too, their difficult achievements — limited, like ours, but available to us if we're interested. They too thought themselves too smart for their own good; they too thought themselves cursed by wised-up meta-consciousness: indeed, it was one of their favourite themes. MacDonogh needs to be looked at again. Retrieval can resolve much, even in an age of humoristic deconstruction, and the ecstasy and frustration of an occluded talent can have the power of shaming a fluent posterity accustomed to much greater exposure. A good part of his example, paradoxically, will lie in his built-in 'obsolescence'; also in the amateurish, extra-curricular, unfinished air which, innocent of calculation and bright with idiosyncrasies (prosodic slippages, late jokes best overlooked, an addiction to 'w' sounds), confirms the authenticity of the enterprise. But *caveat emptor*: too often, revisiting the past with sophisticated hindsight and superior technical means, we lose the original aura, the poignant sense of imperfect, lost reality; we cease to 'walk unaware'. So much the worse for us if we can no longer praise without irony, as MacDonogh does in a prose piece, 'Out of the Night' (*The Dublin Magazine*, 1958), those things, real or imagined, to whose dispersal his own work stands as such courageous testimony: 'religious faith, love between man and woman, nobility of conduct, unexplained gaiety of heart, order and beauty in the natural world'.

Derek Mahon

One Landscape Still

Abroad in wild moon-baronies now swear
With a rich music and expanding thought
To rouse the intellect, delight the ear,
Making a verse meticulously wrought,
Impersonally splendid. Swear to express
The complicated movements of our dust,
Folly of pity, irony of love, and loveliness
Of temporal voices singing because they must
Utter the wonder of intaken breath.
Singing because the certainty of death
Makes life miraculous and youth a glory,
Makes of the antics of man's mind a dress
Rehearsal for some proud fantastic story
As yet unwritten . . . Move from moon-coloured air;
Enter the curtained room; take up the pen;
Choose from bright images a coupling pair,
Begetters of new song . . . And then? . . . What then?

Iambics with a witch's five-fold curse
Make each new child the spit of his last brother —
A ruminative heavy-featured verse,
No more itself than germane to some other
Creature of circumstance. One landscape still! —
Memorial acres, old demented trees
About a crumbling house, a stony hill,
A solitary lake — forever these
Restrict the image and impose their will
To hold the travelling thought. Sun's opening eye

Brightens on water-hens and crested grebes,
A sparkling page of Aristophanes!
But night includes in one tormented cry
Troy and the Greeks and the whole tale of Thebes.

Now the Holy Lamp of Love

Now the holy lamp of love,
Or unholy if they will,
Lifts her amber light above
Cornamona's hill.
Children playing round about
Decent doors at edge of dark
Long ago have ceased to shout.
Now the fox begins to bark.

Cradling hands are all too small
And your hair is drenched with dew;
Love though strong can build no wall
From the hungry fox for you.
Holy men have said their say
And those holy men are right,
God's own fox will have his way
This night or some other night.

Soon with the Lilac Fades Another Spring

Lord! how this rain-sweet greenness shakes the heart
    After untimely drought, after love's lenten fast,
Seeing the tender brightness push apart
    Brown walls of winter. Now to my thoughts at last
Love I have long desired, as grass desires the rain,
    Returns, returns, returns: soft as a settling bird
    Turning itself in the nest, softly her name has stirred —
But oh! this new-sprung joy is all shot through with pain.

This is the self-same wood whose branches wept
    When Deirdre danced to Naisi, these tall trees
Wound aching arms above while Grainne slept,
    And the immortal changeling Héloïse,
Breaking these brilliant pools with naiad feet,
    Ran to her god, suddenly desolate,
    Remembering Paris and the dark house hushed with hate;
Then the long anguish took them, and the Paraclete.

Soon with the lilac fades another spring,
    And one less left to live, and all our springs must die;
In all the world there lives no lasting thing,
    No thing in all the world, and you and I,
Mere ghostly springs of summers long since dead,
    Turn to our winter with no later spring —
    I have no solace from remembering
How death's cold hands will hold that arrogant head.

The old men's bat-like voices on the walls
    Were hushed when Helen passed; and even yet
Across three thousand years that shadow falls
    Upon the face of love, for men forget
No beauty branded with the mark of Cain
    Though all the thoughtless-happy fade apace —
    See, the pale virgin in the chapel-face
Bids the young eyes of spring witness eternal pain.

The Bone-Bright Tree

Six-acre stubble fields provide
In silence of this winter night
No inspiration and no guide
For impregnation of those white
Virginal sheets that wait the pen;
Romantic moonlight can indite
No commentary fit for men
Who mourn that all the best have died
And none conversable is left
To start a dream, or crack a side.
Gone is the courteous acumen,
The wit whose wound was a delight,
The scholar's accuracy worn
Like a bright feather to adorn
Opportune foolery. Bereft,
The sad survivor must abide
His own, or lesser, company
As naked as this bone-bright tree.

This bone-bright tree might still become
A symbol, intricate yet crisp,
Of that once loved astringency,
Before its discipline falls dumb
Under the leaves' insistent lisp —
Summon a spectre, bone-bright tree!
Call up one ghost of all that crowd
(So many gods, no room for men!)
And let him tell at last, out loud,
The secret that impelled him when
He put to sea without a shroud.

What memories in the branches stir?
'So many gods, no room for men,'
Petronius said it and this ghost,
Translator of the Arbiter,
Betrayed his admiration most
By his last imitation; then
With knife and water, as with pen
And strict articulation, he
Ended his sentence perfectly.

Only impertinence could dwell
On thoughts of motive or excuse;
The form is its own parable.
The function of the arbiter
Rests in the skilled and perfect use
Of his select material —
And if the known should seem to be
Devoid of further interest, he
Must go to seek it otherwhere;
So be it by the knife, or noose,
Or at the bottom of the sea,
Himself his executioner.

Incomparable ghost! describe
What hells of boredom you have found.
Do your eternal ears imbibe
Unending, low, insistent sound —
Stale stories whispered in a shell?
Tell, too, your active part in hell.

'Living, my pleasure was to teach
To every living thought a chaste
Completion of expression; mine
Was the quintessence of good taste,

And I imposed a crystalline
Ice-cold precision upon speech.
Mine, too, the instantaneous art
Beyond premeditation, for
I spoke perfection from the heart.
I know that I am damned, because
My style is gone. I move through swarms
Of inarticulate feelings and,
Promiscuous from clause to clause,
My uncontrolled expression warms
To gross excitement, plays the whore
To every chance idea. See — !'
With upraised, fleshless, delicate hand
He touched a twig. The bone-bright tree
Burst in a blaze of flaming leaves,
Then died to silence and the moon.

And still the sad survivor grieves
Mourning lost comrades late and soon.

No Mean City

Though naughty flesh will multiply
Our chief delight is in division;
Whatever of Divinity
We all are Doctors of Derision.
Content to risk a far salvation
For the quick coinage of a laugh
We cut, to make wit's reputation,
Our total of two friends by half.

Nothing More

A primrose by a river's brim
A yellow primrose was to him,
And it was nothing more.

More than essential primrose? Gauge
Of egoistic heresy?
Symbol of sweet humility?
Parable for that botcher, Age,
To smudge the virgin schoolboy's page
With turgid intimations? Or
Mere pin-point of poetic war?

Thick-ankled, smug, pedantic man,
We mocked his slow self-centred thought —
Swallows become pedestrian,
His own dew-drinking stallion brought
To drag a travelling salesman's van
Stocked with morality's pure food
To make us wise, to keep us good.

Oh, we were good and we were wise,
Deriding prudence, when we drew
Brave knowledge in at hands and eyes,
And butterflied whole summers through,
With grave and gentle pauses too.

But I, apostate, worse not better
Than he with his damned primrose, I,
Lapsed protestant of hand, of eye,
Tease testaments from thorn and tree,

Make mountains out of mouse or fly,
And, lost for law behind the letter,
Decline delivery of delight
A generous world consigns to me
With manifests of day and night.

There was a garden once I knew
But I would have it something more.
Fabulous flowers blazed and blew
Fed by a thought, co-adjutor
Of sun and rain and dung and dew
And sweat my diligent flesh would pour
To make a beauty fit for you.

Night-long the fragrant tumult mounts
From trumpet-tongued and thronged racemes;
Day with uncounted flowers accounts
The garden still the thing it seems —
But nothing more! Though flowers live on,
Some real, some inexplicit grace
Forsook the body of the place
Finding that you were gone.

Revaluation

Now I remember nothing of our love
So well as the crushed bracken and the wings
Of doves among dim branches far above —
Strange how the count of time revalues things!

The Widow of Drynam

I stand in my door and look over the low fields of Drynam.
No man but the one man has known me, no child but the one
Grew big at my breast, and what are my sorrows beside
That pride and that glory? I come from devotions on Sunday
And leave them to pity or spite, and though I who had music
    have none
But crying of seagulls at morning and calling of curlews at
    night,
I wake and remember my beauty and think of my son
Who would stare the loud fools into silence
And rip the dull parish asunder.

Small wonder indeed he was wild with breeding and beauty
And why would my proud lad not straighten his back from
    the plough?
My son was not got and I bound in a cold bed of duty
Nor led to the side of the road by some clay-clabbered lout!
No, but rapt by a passionate poet away from the dancers
To curtains and silver and firelight.
O wisely and gently he drew down the pale shell of satin
And all the bright evening's adornment and clad me
Again in the garment of glory, the joy of his eyes.

I stand in my door and look over the low fields of Drynam
When skies move westward, the way he will come from the
    war;
Maybe on a morning of March when a thin sun is shining
And starlings have blackened the thorn,

He will come, my bright limb of glory, my mettlesome wild
    one,
With coin in his pocket and tales on the tip of his tongue;
And the proud ones that slight me will bring back forgotten
    politeness
To see me abroad on the roads with my son,
The two of us laughing together or stepping in silence.

Song

She spoke to me gently with words of sweet meaning,
　　Like the damsel was leaning on Heaven's half-door,
And her bright eyes besought me to leave off deceiving
　　And trouble the parish with scandal no more.

And there, for a moment, I thought I'd be better
　　To take those round arms for a halter and live
Secure and respectable, safe in her shelter,
　　And be the bright pattern of boys in the village.

But I thought how the lane would have sheltering shadows
　　And a glass on the counter would look as before,
And the house was too dark, and her eyes were too narrow,
　　So I left her alone at her door.

From Fields of Sorrow

Wandering these well-loved fields from wood to wood
And small duck-haunted lakes, I have asked myself
Why they are seldom seen apart from sorrow,
And put the thought away. But now I will make
Talk of the thing and leave untouched that shelf
From which, when the old house is still, I take
Book after book and hope in vain to borrow
Cures for the trouble of unruly blood.

O melancholy landscape that I love!
Low-lying fields whose long horizons hold
No shelter from the watchful sky above,
No heights to lessen its immensity,
What sorrow broods, what nameless grief untold
Asks with dumb patience for response from me?
That old wind-broken body of a tree
By the slow river's bend knows more than I
Whether in us you breed the epitome
Of the long quarrel between earth and sky
That will not finish till our star is cold.

Maybe his land absorbs man's history
As a house will, and makes his story plain
That wise and sympathetic men may see
Peace where peace was, and in earth's misery
The emanation of long-buried pain.
These fields, though far, are still continuous
With Innishannon's plain and with the sod
That banks Boyne water, one with Lord Edward Street
And pavements Pearse and Tom MacDonogh trod!

There's blood enough to chill far-wandering feet,
And names enough for winds to whisper us
That even strangers catch. But that's not all!
The fields of France, huge and indifferent,
Bury their dead, and fragrant twilights fall
Ghostless in Piedmont. Something more is meant.
Maybe a land takes on its character
As much from those it breeds as they from it,
And more than mortal tragedy may stir
The grass that blows above the famine pit.
Doomed to unrest we were the fertile soil
In which the promise of eternity
Of peace in God took root. Subtle, trefoil,
Complex in us the Triple Unity
Displaced the grass, the copper and the yew.
Earth's innocent certainties our fathers knew
Were named our enemies: cold shadows fell
On field and flower that have not lifted yet,
Though every leaf in holy Derry lit
The love of angels and the Intangible
Breathed in created beauty. Our disease
Ripens beneath the consciousness of sin:
We are a race whose eyes are turned within
To seek perfection and all mysteries
That draw the mind from what lies next the hand;
Our hope is riddled by the intricacies
Of ever-worming thought — and yet, and yet
We, the inheritors of centuries
Of mystic contemplation, still regret
The loved appearance. Bywords in every land
For devilment and mirth and reckless wit,
We can create no comfortable mind,
No way to heal the imagined enmities
Of spirit and its flesh; there is not a town

But knows our blasphemy, the dreadful lie
We tell to our tormentors when we drown
Thought in debauchery — but on that stair,
Where others find their wit, we pause to find
Our images defaced, and in despair
We lift imploring hands, and the loud cry
Of Faustus breaks upon the bitter air:
I'll leap up to my God, who pulls me down.
Exiled from peace, we neither live nor die.

Exiled from peace! And thought and book are vain,
The ancient quarrel in the blood returns.
Round the dark house the low fields breathe in pain;
Irrational and unassuageable grief
Touches the forehead with the falling leaf.
Yet, looking for cause, the spirit only learns
Tricks of the moonlight and impending rain —
There's nothing but imagination here,
Personal sorrow and a thought-sick brain
That makes all subject to its private fear,
And would have all men sleepless because I
Endure this argument without relief,
This endless quarrel between earth and sky.

Lost Secrecy

Rueful self-knowledge wrecks your smile
In gay disaster, and your eye
Brightens with tender mockery
Of us and our romantic love.
Maternally the watchful dove
Of pity fed its infancy,
But old experience, mile on mile,
Waits for those fledgling wings to try
Deserts of cold hostility.

Lovely those hours and free from fear
Filched from an unsuspecting world,
But now its watchful eye picks out
Which way our quiet footsteps go
And words, however whispered low,
Ring in its intricately curled
Ubiquitous malignant ear,
And all the huddling housetops shout
A bawdy tale for fools to hear.

Over the Water

Through weeks of this windy April with horror hawking
    reason
Reiterated boasting of thrush and blackbird wakened
Anger and lonely hatred that they in their happy season
Cared less for her lost grieving than rapt unknowing faces
She scanned in brittle streets. But oh! returning soon,
Curlew and plover only were brothers to her sorrow
Crying from lonely tillage to a house of empty rooms,
They and that ragged heron who laboured up to tree-tops
Leaving reed-broken silver before her troubled movements.

May brought the south to mellow April's harsh brightness,
But brought no timid stirring of hope to my darling,
There where the wild duck convoys her young from reedy
    islands
Through narrows wharfed by lilies, she saw their shadows
    darken,
Cruciform on the water when foul birds from the sea
Came in for prey. But I had comfort slogging
Hard roads with marching hundreds, lulling a private grief,
Dulling in rhythmic stupor the fierce assaults of longing
And dreading memory less than lacerated feet.

Though noon will drowse in roses her young days carry
    coolness
Cropped from Meath's dawning acres or stolen from
    shadows
Under Dunboyne's tall hedges that lately shut the moon
From those more lucky lovers whom flitting dusk had
    gathered

In gentle couples. Here skies have scarcely room
To house their clouds of bombers, yet had I but my darling,
We'd mix our hate with pity for stripling airmen doomed
To their own strange damnation, and in a night of horror
Softly we'd lie together under a bomber's moon.

Lothario's Song

The owls are out about the trees
  On silent wing or softly hooting,
And love that swore to be at ease
  Begins his old freebooting;
For every wailing wind's asleep
  And moonlight has a softer shine,
And the townland's sluggard hearts would leap
  To keep so sweet a tryst as mine.

She slips between their dreams of her
  Down to the salleys by the river,
Where only wakeful wildfowl stir
  With a ripple of light and a reedy shiver;
And there, while willows weep above,
  Leaning her whiteness to the bark,
She finds eternity in love
  That dies before the rising lark.

On the Island

Less foreign than a bird
And feckless as a flower,
Here with no human word
I watch from hour to hour
The magical bodies of terns
Fishing a sandy shallow,
Changing from swallow to hawk
And back from hawk to swallow.
Lovers at night will walk
Inland when grasses sigh
And in a windless hollow
Out of the moon's eye
Lover will laugh with lover,
But now no sound alarms
The dreamy hatching plover.
Small spiders stumbling on my arms
Where tangled sunlight burns
Disturb this world as much as I
Who watch the tireless terns
Or, rapt in a child's wonder,
Let all the close-coiled mind
Loosen, as out from under
Pale ferns unwind.

The Injury

I who have hurt you stand accused
By sight and sound: last night I heard
The owl upon his murderous round;
You were the mouse, you were the bird
That he must find, and you the furred
Warm creature that I heard last spring
Crying under the tunnelled beech.
This wind that strips the island birch
Finds you beyond my human reach,
Isled in your leaden lake of pain:
These ruined roses in the rain,
The crooked stone, the roofless church,
Are images of all I do,
And though my laden spirit tries
To wing her usual way to you
She cannot stir, she cannot rise —
And the cold lake's between us two!

This Morning I Wakened Among Loud Cries of Seagulls

This morning I wakened among loud cries of seagulls
Thronging in misty light above my neighbour's ploughland,
And the house in its solid acres was carried wheeling
Encircled in desolate waters and impenetrable cloudy
Wet winds that harried and lost the sea-birds' voices
And the voice of my darling, despairing and drowning,
Lost beyond finding in the bodiless poising
Dissolving shapes of grey mist crowding,
Till the wind grew still and the water noiseless.

Later, when the sun groped down and flung wide open
Mist-hung curtains from laughing brilliant meadows,
Taking my rod I crossed by grassy slopes
To the sunshot river and fished a run of shadows,
But between each take and strike her nervous fingers lightly
Twitched my tense elbow and I missed him, turning
To that beloved face — but, oh sweet Christ,
The shining air was empty! And choked with earth
And roots of grass I gnawed the day to twilight.

Big-boned and breasted like her own timeless mountains
She broke herself to housecraft, groping in crowded shadows,
Nursing a brood of phantoms until her days were shrouded
From warmth of sun or love or help of kindly hands —
And oh white fog had clouded the valleys when I rose,
Had scarfed the water's face and choked the source of twilight;
Owl-hoot and chuck of water-fowl came dropping ghostly
Passing wan hosts of jonquils in the wood where silence
Gathered the grey trunks as I stumbled homeward.

from Intractable

The incipient godhead in the soul
Craved nourishment and was denied,
The flaming mare led on her foal,
Seven score of moons grew up and died,
But still the sun's encyclical
Gilded gaunt housetops all in vain,
The unshriven soul refuses all
The healing sacrament of pain,
Refuses all and rears in pride
Against the embattled skies and calls
Forsaken allies to its side,
Mouthing dead faiths, while ruin falls.

The Wind Cries

The wind cries that we shall walk together
Under heavy green branches and never remember
Our hearts grown big with love and so grief-quickened
That a snowflake could bruise them this dark December.

Afterpeace

This wind that howls about our roof tonight
And tears live branches screaming from great trees
Tomorrow may have scarcely strength to ruffle
The rabbit's back to silver in the sun.

The Dream

How splendidly this dream
Grows big behind the eyes.
Its fibres throng the brain
Whose laboured soil is fed
With humour and delight;
And all the night becomes
One slowly opening flower,
One vast unfolding white
Lily whose climbing light
Heralds the holy dawn.

Dunleary Harbour

Once again, from this debris of rocks, after how many years,
I look down on those ambient arms, that changeless embrace
Of holiday water. Half blinded by tears
I look down, and the pain of disgrace
And my lunatic fears give me peace, give me peace,
For a while in the sun-sleepy silence. How long this release?

How long this release from the troop of unnameable things
Behind the left shoulder, the desolate cry
That swells in the throat, the soft bat-beat of wings
Under belly and breast? Is it I, is it I
Who inhabit this body still cleanly and strong?
Was it spirit or flesh first committed, first suffered the wrong?

Is it I who remember swift boats and spray in the bows,
The flurry of flesh with a girl on the rampart of rocks,
Gargantuan sallies and Shelleyan raptures and vows,
Petrarchan devotion dispersed on the crowing of cocks?
Is it I who remember fierce tensions of language and thought,
And glories infrequent, authentic, vouchsafed though
     unsought?

We had eaten and drunk enough, enough we had played.
It was time to depart when the friends we loved grew wise.
But through fear or folly or common politeness we stayed
To the death of the innocent heart, the end of surprise;
Till light was lost and emptiness grew in the night
And the left hand of silence no longer enquired of the right.

It is time to return from this debris of rocks and of years,
And the image of indolent summer asleep on the bay.
There was healing perhaps in the terrible torrent of tears
That drove me rebellious, a truant for part of one day
From the house in the trees where shadows converse of their
    state
Or, staring at Nothing, for Nothing eternally wait.

Old Eros

Compulsions of the flesh have left him bare
Of all a lonely intellect once planned;
The sensual present found him everywhere
Daft with delight or blind with blood's despair
Thrusting an angel off on either hand.
Flesh on a frame, how should he understand
The old predicament encountered there?
Final defection of intelligence,
The unschooled mind refusing every fence,
The argument that sinks into the sand.

So the few friends folly has not estranged
Nor indolence foregone, endure the show
Of what were thoughts, or works, had flesh been
   kinder,
Articulated anecdotes arranged
In joyless dance, each linked with a reminder
To hold some listener, too polite to go
Out of his boredom's hell, while to and fro
The puppets jerk, and grin, but never grieve.
None joins the cast and none is free to leave
The old blind master growing always blinder.

You, Too, at Midnight Suddenly Awaking

You, too, at midnight suddenly awaking,
Faint with fear lest I be not there,
With timid hand, your heart near breaking,
Felt and found me and did not dare
To wake me, but watched the slow light making
Night's sad mysteries mean and bare.

I was the loved one, you were the lover,
In dim small hours when the scent was blown
Of the sea-salt stinging the too sweet clover,
Yours was the fear lest you woke alone —
Strange, with a sleep or two gone over
I should be finding your fear my own.

Dodona's Oaks were Still

He told the barmaid he had things to do,
Such as to find out what we are and why.
He said, I must have winter in the mountains,
Spring is no good, nor summer,
And even autumn carries too much colour.
I must have winter. Winter's naked line
Is truth revealed and there's a discipline
Along the edges of gaunt rocks on frosty nights.
She said she thought so too,
And so he left
Bookshops and music and the sight of friends,
Good smokeroom laughter starred with epigrams,
Seven sweet bridges and those bucking trams
That blunder west through bitter history,
And women,
Perhaps particularly women,
Climbing like slow white maggots through his thought;
He left the lot,
And got him to a shack above the city,
Lit a white candle to his solitude
And searched among the images he'd seen
Of his own self in other minds to find
Mankind in him.
He hoped to see the whole
Diverse and complicated world
Fold up and pack itself into his soul
The way a walnut's packed.
The lonely fool,
Squatting among the heavy mountain shapes,
Looked on the wet black branches and the red,

Followed the urgent branches to their tips
And back again through twig and stem to root,
Always alone and busy with himself,
Enquiring if this world of decent men
Must be hell's kitchen to the end of time,
Because of that old crime, incorrigible pride,
Strong powers of angels soured by impotence,
Rebellious godhead working its hot way
Through tangled veins.
He cried in pain towards the writhing trees,
But heard no voice.
Dodona's oaks were still.

The Drunkard

I watch him travel happily
    Along the lane's moon-brightened edge,
Heedless of these lovers' low
    Voices in the darker hedge.

Oh, to be drunk or deep in love
    And so forget this empty heart,
And walk more careless than a god
    Or feel the dry thorns prick and start!

O Tardy Spring

Though furtive ice may lurk in shadowy creeks
Green summer lights upon the lake today.
The populous waters wake, emblazoned, gay,
Wave-arrowed by the swan's wake as he seeks
Escaping loveliness. Far fledgling weeds
Rise to the measure of each venomous thrust
That gains him nothing though he throws away
Splendour and dignity; she will not stay!
Lithe and serene she moves beyond the lust
That follows plunging, while with bawdy shrieks
Bald coot and water-hen change partners, play
Rude games of country love, and from close reeds,
Mocking and sly, the nodding drakes survey
This rowdy, rich, Hogarthian holiday.

Slowly the wound that knows no healing bleeds
In me, of all God's kissing creatures here
Alone and loveless. Chaffinch from the dogwood cries
Again, again, one word, and his small dear,
That mite of feathers in the thorn, replies
That he has all her heart and she is near!
O spring, how spend this weight of love that lies
Unuttered in my flesh? O tardy spring,
If spring at all, denying me, who bear
Knowledge of birth and death, this ignorant thing
That bird and beast and the fool primrose share.
The flower's life is sleeplike, yet, aware,
She turns, all eagerness, to take the bee.
And the slow being of the rooted tree
Stirs in his deeps when April's bawdy air

Bears him abroad. Waste that outruns repair
Destroys this body and will change in me
Enormous longing to an old man's sigh.
I am the idle branch, my budless eye
Blinder than cells whose immortality
Was never pawned for love. But I must die!

Be Still as You are Beautiful

Be still as you are beautiful
Be silent as the rose;
Through miles of starlit countryside
Unspoken worship flows
To reach you in your loveless room
From lonely men whom daylight gave
The blessing of your passing face
Impenetrably grave.

A white owl in the lichened wood
Is circling silently,
More secret and more silent yet
Must be your love to me.
Thus, while about my dreaming head
Your soul in ceaseless vigil goes,
Be still as you are beautiful
Be silent as the rose.

Curtain

What high enchantment leaves us then
Alone with those sad thoughts that tear
In silence at the hearts of men
Who know desire begets despair
And know that love in them is dead
Before the frightened stars have fled
The dawn, or the long hair
Is bound again?

Escape to Love

No pride hath he who sings of escape from love:
All songs of escape from love are songs of despair:
Who so hath gat him away hath got nowhere.
— James Stephens

1

In a dark hour this thing began, in a dark house,
The hour when the great wild beast of our time, the
    scrabbling mouse,
Wakens the dreamer to sudden unreasoning dread,
When fires are cold, time shrunken, books dead.
He awoke, as he thought, to the terrible sound of the
    mouse —
Silence. A dead hand silenced the listening house.
And then, like a mouse in the gut, It moved, like a breath,
A flower opening, a whisper of malice, a four-month sin
In a woman's frightened flesh; softly, but certain, within,
Softly it moved, nosing inside him, softly withdrew,
Then returned with a confident tooth, or a claw, and he knew
That the thing living and growing within him was Death.

2

On this, the first bright Sunday of March, he awoke
To birdsong, the first true birdsong of the year.
His mind stirred gladly, then suddenly felt the yoke,
And from the sunny window he turned in fear,

Hearing the ebb-tide turn, hearing huge seas of pain
Beat back towards a soft defenceless shore,
Moaning around the island of sense once more,
And the dry sunlight darkened as with rain.

Last night Vladimir Rosing sang Rachmaninoff,
Sing no sad song, O do not sing again,
And afterwards fire flickered over a floor
Of faded flowers no children's feet shall press
And, dying, it dropped from the smooth handle of
That sad, symbolic, adamantine door
That closed upon him once. There is no redress
For the heart withheld from love, for the wasted
    hours and weeks
That grow to be years, while the power to love grows less,
Till a dead man rises and goes to his work, and a ghost
    speaks.

But this is Sunday when the dead are free to be dead,
Free to study their death and to watch themselves decay.
For three thin days of thaw after a six-weeks' frost
Wet winds were blowing a blind mist overhead
That dripped from the blackened buds. But now great sun
    is up
And all the world should rejoice. But for him this is a day
Of darkening symbols, when nothing is merely itself;
For innocent things as they are require an innocent mind,
And it's long since we were children, the books unread on
    the shelf,
A painted dog to delight in the base of the emptied cup,
And wonder no less wonderful though hardly found when
    lost,
For whatever today took from us tomorrow had more to
find

And the thing found was a good thing though it went like
   breath in frost.

3

Lugete, O lugete, Veneres —
Idle capacity, indefensible waste,
Love's measureless potential wasting unused!
Mother of Rimbaud, weep for what you have done,
Weep for small outstretched arms that you refused,
Weep for the pains you could, but would not, ease.
But here's no Rimbaud — this one has never tried
To share God's throne, pursue the alchemical gold
In crucibles of debauch. No supernatural son
Walks the brown stubble now. Now as the buds unfold
Your frosty duty nips, heart holds sour aftertaste
Of chilly nurture. In your chaste heaven remember
How, to be wise, you trained your gentleness
To acrimonious care and, to be strong, denied
Love's only eloquent proof, the irrational caress.
Years of this heart hold no month but December.

4

Heartlessly, O heartlessly, the larks rise up uncaring,
Out of the brown stubble the larks rise up and sing.
Their heartless coloratura wakens a heartless spring
   To blossom and blow uncaring, as though time stored no ill
For our doomed breed that goes to sleep despairing,
   And wakes despairing still.

Faithfully, O faithfully, the stubborn sense recovers
The gay confiding innocence that rose to greet the spring,
Before ironic time had taught that name to plant a sting
  In man who rediscovers his need of love too late
And among foes that should be friends and lovers
  Follows his loveless fate.

5

Having no dog he is come by poisoned lands
(Ten silly sheep of Mongan's in one night)
To where the unwanted lovely column stands
Of the old mill, disgraced and wingless now.
Time-silvered timbers tumbled on its brow
Hang witlessly; yet, stature and dignity impress
Featureless land, as some old labourer might,
Great though bewildered in his dumb distress,
Still dominate the fields he used to plough.
Smooth-handed, literate, this later victim knows
Not time's ingratitude for work well done
But shame of the unlaboured self. Deathward he goes,
Too cold to have bred a maggot in the sun,
Ghost among ghosts he has allowed to pass
Without one gesture to the loneliest one.

Climbing the hill he felt the bone in the ground,
Under the thaw, under the springing grass,
And thought how always in good verse he had found
The intellectual bone under the lyric line,
But in great verse much more. And how he had failed,
Lacking the stature demanded by Mallarmé's
Imperious phrase that puts mere talent in place —

Greatness of soul. At least he had had the grace
Not to dissemble with truth, never availed
Of spurious comfort drawn from uncritical praise,
But doubted and, doubting, knew the infallible sign
Had left him unmarked. Achievement offered no sop
To rueful self-knowledge, but courage could gaze
Unabashed at the beautiful brickwork dead at the top,
And careless of all but the sweet discipline
Could think of Dunbar, could grin and agree
Timor mortis conturbat me.

6

Alone and Godless, stopped by the sudden edge
Of the great quarry slicing the limestone height,
He sees, as from his own life's ultimate ledge,
Symbols of fear and love where slow black families
Creep home from church, home from huge mysteries,
From terrible love home to love's kitchen cares.
New sense of isolation, unawares,
Half-opens doors to dim divinities,
To his unwelcome godhead thrust out of sight
By a long indolent act of sacrilege.
He, the unsatisfied, hating the arid light,
Uncharmed, that lit the scrubbed boards of one creed,
Refused the encumbered heritage, loaded with doubt,
Half-envying, half-despising these poor heirs
Enriched by faith. Political orphan, too,
Fouled by his forebears' history he knew
Himself the enemy of that narrow breed,
But no friend to the breed that threw them out.

7

Below in the sun-dazed field there's something stirs —
Two God-fed Christians, freed for sweet Sunday sport,
Each with his murderous hound. Deep in the bursting furze
The dogs are suddenly slipped — Oh, but the start is short!
Apex of all earth's inescapable woes
The ousted hare streaks for the corner hedge
And death's sharp angle narrows to its close.

High on a lost world's last and perilous edge
Blind sympathy of flesh shared the expected hell
Of that warm palpitant body torn apart;
Blind instinct to save ran into empty air,
Two hundred feet of it, and as he fell
(Who knows the ingredients of a miracle?)
Wire in the gapped hedge saved the uncaptured hare.

Silence of Sunday. Nothing moves anywhere
But lazy seagulls away in the azure above
This small impacted muddle of blood and bone
Motionless in the sun's unblinking stare.
Anticipation of long pain endured alone
All groundless now, blinded by sudden love,
Loveless too long, he has plunged to the matter's heart —
Love's ultimate kindness on a bed of stone.

Waking

Peace, there is peace in this awaking.
Slowly, silently the warm sun
Enters my being. Waves are breaking,
Unseen as time, one after one
Endlessly breaking. A seagull crying
Voices eternity. There stirs
A wind among the grass and sighing
Carries my spirit to hers.

Of Late

She is grown old of late, so very still.
Her voice is fallen quiet and her hands
Have lost a little sureness. She is more sparing
Of her known smile that earns a finer strength.
Her eyes are a deep shadow and a dewy light
As though, for ever, they looked back at youth
Or saw new dawns grow bright before their time.

She Walked Unaware

Oh, she walked unaware of her own increasing beauty
That was holding men's thoughts from market or plough,
As she passed by intent on her womanly duties
And she without leisure to be wayward or proud;
Or if she had pride then it was not in her thinking
But thoughtless in her body like a flower of good breeding.
The first time I saw her spreading coloured linen
Beyond the green willow she gave me gentle greeting
With no more intention than the leaning willow tree.

Though she smiled without intention yet from that day
    forward
Her beauty filled like water the four corners of my being,
And she rested in my heart like a hare in the form
That is shaped to herself. And I that would be singing
Or whistling at all times went silently then,
Till I drew her aside among straight stems of beeches
When the blackbird was sleeping and she promised that never
The fields would be ripe but I'd gather all sweetness,
A red moon of August would rise on our wedding.

October is spreading bright flame along stripped willows,
Low fires of the dogwood burn down to grey water —
God pity me now and all desolate sinners
Demented with beauty! I have blackened my thought
In drouths of bad longing, and all brightness goes shrouded
Since he came with his rapture of wild words that mirrored
Her beauty and made her ungentle and proud.
Tonight she will spread her brown hair on his pillow,
But I shall be hearing the harsh cries of wild fowl.

Flowering Currant

From plum-tree and cherry
White blossom froths over.
The small birds make merry
And each is a lover.

But she walks by a tree
And a spring-quickened bird
Which her eyes do not see
And her ears have not heard.

For her ears hear only
The cold voice within
That wars on her lonely
Delight, and her sin.

And her looks ever bend
To the path at her feet
Lest she see to the end
Where the combatants meet.

Delight and despair
In the bright currant blossom
His lips on her hair
His hands at her bosom,

His hands at her breast,
His lips on her hair
Saying, 'Rest you, now rest
From fasting and prayer.

My floor is not stone,
My couch is no board;
And what loss is but one
Of his brides to the Lord?'

O, Come to the Land

O, come to the land of the saint and the scholar
Where learning and piety live without quarrel,
Where the coinage of mind outvalues the dollar
And God is the immanent shaper of thought and behaviour;
Where old ceremonious usage survives as the moral
And actual pattern of grace, where the blood of our Saviour
Is real as our sin, and replenishes spirit and brain
Till they blossom in pity and love as our fields in the rain.

No, but come to a land where the secret censor
Snouts in the dark, where authority smothers
The infant conscience and shadows a denser
Darkness on ignorant minds in their tortuous groping
For spectreless day: a land where austerity mothers
The coldly deliberate sins, where harsh masters are roping
The heels of the heavenly horse and blinding the bright
Incorruptible eye that dares open in passionless light.

O, come to the land where man is yet master
Of tyrannous time and will pause for the pleasure
Of speech or of sport though worldly disaster
Pluck at torn sleeves; a land where soft voices
Meet answering laughter, where the business of living is
    leisure,
Where there's no heart so poor but it's kindly and quick and
    rejoices
In horse or in hound or the mettlesome boy with a ball,
Where a jibe's for the proud, but a hand's for the helpless
    from all.

No, but come to a land where the mediaeval
Dread of the woman mutters in corners,
Thunders from pulpits, where the only evil
Lacking forgiveness is love; a land where the spirit
Withers the flowering flesh, where whispering mourners
Crowd to the grave of romance and expect to inherit
Great scandalous wealth to lighten long evenings and bring
A venomous joy to harsh lips whose kiss is a sting.

O, come to the land where imagination
Fashions the speech of the common people
Rich as a tenement's shattered mouldings
Where the wrong of defeat has bequeathed to a nation
Ironic traditional wit, like a polished steeple
Rising precise and clear from the huddled holdings
Of intricate minds that, in face of Eternity, know
Harsh humour and absolute faith their sole strongholds
    below.

No, but come to a land where the dying eagle
Is mocked by the crow and the patient vulture,
Where nobility fails and the ancient regal
Pride of inheritance yields to the last invaders —
Image and hare-brained song, the scum of an alien culture
Bubbling in village and street, where unmannerly traders
And politic slaves have supplanted the gentle and brave,
Where the hero will never have honour except in the grave.

The Frozen Garden

Already the early year has brought more than one morning
When the poor clerk leaving his doorstep has stopped,
Perplexed by the mind's sudden lightness,
And stood staring
At the moist sky and the brilliant drops
A-row on the railing, and a sparrow swaying
In sooty privet, and called through the hallway
For his wife to come to the doorway's brightness and stand
Aproned and wiping her wet hands,
Smelling the soft air, nodding and saying,
As a new surprising and personal thing,
'How mild it is,' and 'Just like spring.'

And to us, loving a garden, certain days have been
The best of our year that come, unexpected, between
These frozen February days and bring
A sudden soft expectancy of spring —
Days when the mind turns busily over
The promise of planned shapes and colours
Prompted by green treasures,
Discovered shoots under black pulp of leaves,
Marks a new sureness in the blackbird's note and measures
New thickness in the daffodil, and once again believes
The truth of resurrection, knows the brute
Has failed in final conquest of the lover.

Will it ever be so again? Will the expectation
Of personal pleasure, indulged for a moment, escape
Conviction of guilt?
Frost holds the garden now in a stillness of crystalline shape,

A lovely negation
Of living, which winter has built
On the structure of life itself; but deep in the clay
Strong roots bide their time,
Using delay
To gather and hoard from the soil strength to endure:
Whatever is doubtful the coming of spring is sure.

Whatever is doubtful the coming of spring is sure.
We have heard the tentative thrush,
We have heard . . . we have heard
Swart men looking up from maps on the table,
Looking in each other's eyes, nodding and saying,
'When the spring comes . . .' O magic word,
Instinct with life, when the lovely fable
Renews itself, and Persephone,
Pale from the shadowy months, comes up, what will she see?
She will falter and turn and beg for the wastes of hell:
They have planned so well.

'Consider the hosts of pale moon-flower faces swaying
Fathoms deep in dim tides that heave and stir,
Rooted among rocks at the ocean's bed.
Consider the newly dead whom the seas prefer!
Consider,' the thrush said,
'How lightfoot soon over our bright green western sod,
From primrose woods April comes dancing to scatter
The flowers of our childhood — O God! O God!'
Sang the thrush,
'I see strange flowers of red and white suddenly spatter
Our innocent acres, and strange birds wheeling,
I see brimmed wine, bread broken, but nobody kneeling.'

They have planned it well; they say it with proper pride,
'Your darkest dreams are nothing to set beside
The glories we bring you in spring' —
The mindless men behind wire,
The good brain crushed by a heel,
The wolfish nightmare children, these we shall not forget,
Nor your villages bombed in the sun, your cities screaming
    in fire,
The tramp of feet in the night, the glitter of moonlit steel —
Wait for it, wait for the spring, and the terrible years will
    seem
Remote and still as the garden's frozen dream.

War Widow

These are the self-same ways you walked, crazy with grief,
Waking this sleeping water to hear your stumbling woes,
Blind with importunate tears when the wild duck rose from
    the lake,
And hoping your heart might break before the fall of the leaf.
But sight was stark in the dawn, and the heart refused to break,
And, thronged or alone, it ached until, with the star-bright
    sloes,
The pains of the dying year were lost in the pangs of spring
And, breaking from blinding lilies, the clamorous drake
    arose —
But the wild duck moaned in the ozier bed, spreading a
    wounded wing.

These are the willow boughs that wept, casting wild shade,
When, with protesting murmurs, you saw in love's disguise
The face of the warring world, as the moon came over the hill,
And the individual heart, the innocent life betrayed
By nobleness of mind serving a brutal will.
Then the quivering branch was still, and stillness grew in
    your eyes,
Struggling no more against grief and, lifting your listening
    head
To hear the wild duck moaning, you laughed your gay good-
    byes,
From a heart that you hoped was dying to a love already dead.

Break no more from the willow branch emblems of grief,
For you that were death's rival must take a live love soon,
Drowning in curtained laughter the wild duck's endless
    moan,
And walking no more alone in woods where a falling leaf
Brings him again from the sky who journeyed proud and
    alone,
Doomed like the conquering drone, shattered in blazing
    noon —
Give him again to death! for your time draws near to break
This grief-charmed ghostly circle, your six-years' honeymoon,
And the dead leaves mixed in the waking earth fell for the
    live leaf's sake.

The Snare

He stoops above the clumsy snare
To take the night's yet living loot,
When the wild creature kicking there
Beside the thorn-tree's tunnelled root
Flings up red soil into his eyes —
And suddenly the April skies
Are loud with pain of man and brute,
Until he lifts a clabbered boot
And stamps red life into the sod,
And silence takes the fields again —
The old deceptive peace of God!

Courtesy

She was a creature all impulsive heart
And all her wit was in the ways of love —
Wit without wisdom or the conscious art
To fill the gaps in feeling. The more she strove
The more he wearied of the one poor part
Her innocence had learned: until satiety
Became fastidious, proud in continence —
Then all her loveliness, with no defence,
Died in the savage airs of courtesy.

Feltrim Hill

The land around is all so flat
That Feltrim makes a noted hill
And you may look far out to sea
Standing beside the mill.

Here, once, by hedged and dusty lanes
The rustling acres made their way
And none who met but blessed the load
And passed the time of day.

Within the shadow of this arch
The miller watched to see them climb,
The white dust drifted in the sun
As to the end of time.

The ploughman at Kinsaley stood
To watch the lumbering sails go round,
Then turned contented to his toil
Knowing whose corn was ground.

Lovely and strong these wine-dark walls
Preserve intact their circle still,
But time has wrung that wheel of life
Whose hub was Feltrim Mill.

The sails of forty feet are gone,
The dome is fallen, and on high
The great rack bares its idle fangs
Against a cruel sky.

And when they blast the hill beneath
The aged timber leaps and groans,
The flesh of plaster falls away
Leaving the naked bones.

The quarry eats into the hill,
The hungry lorries come and go,
And Feltrim Hill itself will pass
Into the roads below.

Helen

No one escapes you — certainly not we who thought
You had passed scornfully by because we beat
A little ball about green fields, and we had caught
The time's quick-jigging madness, the loud deceit
Of a new music forever crying in its madness —
Let reel the drunken notes, your beauty still broke
   through!
Then we turned to shelter from you in false sadness,
In pictured tales of troubled lives, but you
Make sorrow of our sadness. You in the long nights tell
What dreaming rage impelled the Grecian boats,
For you are the limbs' delight, the spirit's hell,
The pity of Christ and the broken horns of the goats!

The River

Stir not, whisper not,
Trouble not the giver
Of quiet who gives
This calm-flowing river,

Whose whispering willows,
Whose murmuring reeds
Make silence more still
Than the thought it breeds,

Until thought drops down
From the motionless mind
Like a quiet brown leaf
Without any wind;

It falls on the river
And floats with its flowing,
Unhurrying still
Past caring, past knowing.

Ask not, answer not,
Trouble not the giver
Of quiet who gives
This calm-flowing river.

Marriage Song

Curlews cry imploringly
Out in the unmeasured dark.
Sleepy coops uneasily
Hear the hungry foxes bark.
But this night's less dangerous
Than the day which threatens us
With a light we know too well —
O, discover deep in me
Wells of peace accessible
To your sick humanity.

Brood no more on memory;
Even our dearest newly-dead
Have forgotten us, and we
Soon enough shall share that bed.
We, though not gregarious,
Must devote our over-plus
Of eternity to them;
So, unsummoned, let them lie
Till our life's last apothegm
Names us of their company.

2

Greedily the living wait
To prey upon our time and thought,
And leave no room to correlate
What we would with what we ought.
Well-intentioned friends intrude
On self-sufficing solitude
With daily triviality.
But this night we dedicate,
In darkness and in privacy,
To a truth beyond debate.

Free of the living and the dead
Forget awhile our share of shame:
For hearts that break, for blood that's shed
The individual man's to blame —
We know it in our helplessness
And as we wake and rise and dress
We reassume a guilty world.
But tonight the Doom's unsaid,
The wings of the Avenger furled;
Impassioned Peace protects this bed.

The Rust is on the Lilac Bloom

The rust is on the lilac bloom
And on the hinges of my mind.
Break in upon that quiet room,
Pull back the curtains, lift the blind —
Victorian brass all tarnished now,
Worm in the good mahogany.
Come, most meticulous *hausfrau*,
Refurbish all there's left to see.

But when you scrub and scour the mind
For God's sake leave the heart alone,
For there most certainly you'll find
No more than Yeats' foul rag and bone —
Beings whose blood no longer beats,
Sweet masks from which the flesh is gone.
Your concentration still defeats
The images it broods upon.

Far from Ben Bulben

The daffodils are out again
Under the pregnant chestnut buds;
They do not mitigate this pain
That whispers from the greasy suds
Among the dishes in the sink.
Sleep and forget! Awake and think
How the chaste maid is shamed again
In gaudy treacheries of drink
And hopes of monetary gain.
The plea is *Guilty* still, m'luds,
Sentence, *Oblivion's endless clink.*

Nobility once more there were
If somehow from the noise and stink
Arose a second to declare
Justification on this brink
Of nothing. One with poise
Pitched halfway between love and hate,
Arrogant poet, well aware
How the acknowledged legislate
Yet how — the legal mind's despair —
The intellectual celibate
Must mix his thought with strange alloys,
Passion and dream, to fabricate
Unageing monuments. Ah boys!
Who'll wake the dead at Clonmacnoise?

Sworn to accidia we proclaim
Cold cerebration paramount,
Gestures without affection's aim,
Always a falsified account
With neither heart nor soul laid bare
But balanced figures everywhere.
Beware! Wise innocent, beware
This gelid eye, this thinning hair,
Beware this unimpassioned will,
This far too studious aftercare
Of every stillborn oracle.

Shock

Love, like a broken eagle, falls
Among the stones of daily life.
Two dream-fed lovers stare appalled
And know themselves for man and wife.

First Truth

Elucidate your truth for me.
How can I know you who behold
Only the bright periphery?
Essentially unbought, unsold,
You yield your unrevealing kiss.
Not me your secret arms enfold
Though truthfully you murmur, 'This
Is an embodied truth you hold.'

I could forego the embodied truth
With all its warmth if I could find
The secret that your frightened youth
Buried one midnight in your mind.
If I could find first truth in you,
Let it be alien, cold, unkind,
I'd change it for this residue,
This bulk that leaves the spirit blind.

Make Believe

Staring from the square of scullery window
Pretend, if you will, that the hungry shrubs
Are Stickillen's beeches, that twelve yards of grass
Are wind-waving meadows and the dried-up bubs
On the dying lilac are milky with springs
Of a time that was.

Make believe, if you will, that young women tottering
On high stilettoes, in a hurry to the bus,
Are finicky plover running in the stubbles
Around Stabannon; see the house opposite us
As that shack in the forest, our Enchanted Castle,
Long before these troubles.

But, staring in at the same old questions,
Never pretend that convictions of truth,
Those prizes of ignorance, can be won again
With all the knowing solutions of youth,
But turn to each other, glad of the reality,
And accept the pain.